The High-Sexuality Diet

Have you been on so many diets that you can barely remember when you bought your first container of cottage cheese – or even why? Have you jogged around the block so many times in your track suit and leg warmers that even the dogs don't bother chasing you any more? Are you slim and trim now, but limp and listless as well? Are you still plumpish and have trouble seeing your toes yet alone touching them? Perhaps it is time for a new and sexier you. . . .

Ever since Eve invited Adam to share her apple there has been a connection between food and sex that even fast-food chains and processed foods haven't been able to obliterate totally. Today nutritionists and sexologists would largely agree that sexuality is closely allied with nutrition and good health. THE HIGH-SEXUALITY DIET incorporates not only good nutrition and a diet designed for high-energy and maximum health and vitality, but makes it fun as well. Fun and sexy. Here is a diet that will improve your spirits as much as your health.

Ursula Lecordier
The High-Sexuality Diet

ARROW BOOKS

To MLZ

Arrow Books Limited
17–21 Conway Street, London W1P 6JD

An imprint of the Hutchinson Publishing Group

London Melbourne Sydney Auckland
Johannesburg and agencies throughout the world

First published 1984

© Ursula Lecordier 1984

This book is sold subject to the condition that it shall not, by way of trade or otherwise, be lent, resold, hired out, or otherwise circulated without the publisher's prior consent in any form of binding or cover other than that in which it is published and without a similar condition including this condition being imposed on the subsequent purchaser

Set in VIP Bembo by
D. P. Media Limited, Hitchin, Hertfordshire
Printed and bound in Great Britain by
Anchor Brendon Limited, Tiptree, Essex

ISBN 0 09 934760 1

Contents

Introduction 7
1 The secrets of aphrodisiacs 11
2 The miracle/beauty foods 18
3 Beauty formulas 24
4 Beauty cocktails 29
5 The high-sexuality diet 31
6 Switch-on breakfasts 36
7 Hot soups 38
8 Overtures: Hors-d'oeuvres, salads and chutneys à la fantasmagorique 48
9 Lovable lunches 58
10 Intimate dinners 64
11 Sinful sweets 81
12 Before and after drinks 88
13 Exercises 95
14 Oriental massage 106
15 Vitamin chart 112
16 Calorie and fibre counter 115
17 List of suppliers 119
18 Weights and measures 122
   Index 124

Acknowledgements

I would like to thank Mr M Naiken, herbalist in Port-Louis, Mauritius, for letting me into some of his secrets about aphrodisiacs; Mr Henry Bheeka and his family for allowing me to use their charming cottage in the beautiful setting of Riche-en-Eau, Mauritius to write the book; and Elizabeth Mann, first British champion gymnast, for her help with the exercises.

I am also very grateful to *Woman's Journal*, the Morlé Slimming and Beauty Clinic, Semra Gulbakar of the London Institute of Beauty, Bruno Tourail, Dyan Sheldon, Armand Bheeka-Lemasson and Solange Souris.

Introduction

Your mother probably told you (as her mother told her) that the way to a man's heart is through his stomach. Truer words were never spoken – and in more ways than one. For ever since Eve invited Adam to share her apple there has been a connection between food and sex that even fast-food chains and frozen dinners cannot totally hide. Food is more than nourishment. For though the right foods are obviously crucial to building both a strong, healthy body and a strong, healthy mind, and necessary for a personal sense of well-being, food is also a comfort and a celebration. The sharing of food is a serious and joyous proposition; the eating of it a richly and continuously sensual experience. Remember the taste of those first blackberries and the way the juice ran down your chin? Remember the aroma of your mother's special stew? Remember the indescribably delicious cheese and biscuits you and your first great love used to nibble in bed?

These days, many of us not only eat the wrong foods and too much of them, but eat hastily and unthinkingly – grabbing a quick sandwich lunch or a slapdash supper simply to stop our hunger, stuffing our mouths with boring and un-nutritional snacks when there is nothing else to do – more as though we were animals feeding than people indulging in one of man's (and woman's) greatest and most gratifying pleasures. Special diets, also, whether specifically for weight loss or simply for healthy eating, have done much to de-romanticize and trivialize the ritual of eating and the importance of food. Largely conceived as exercises in discipline and self-control, traditional diets give no thought at all to the pleasures, the romance and the sheer fun of food. Food, after all, stimulates more than cell growth. Indeed, many a wan and worn-out dieter will tell you how difficult it is to think of a night of unbridled lust and passion (no matter how much better those black slacks are fitting, no matter how much healthier looking the hair and nails) when meals offer all the excitement and magic of a jog around the block in the rain. On the other hand, of course, it would be just as difficult to find someone who had been seduced over a plate of bangers and mash as over a soy burger and a bowl of lettuce with lemon.

The high-sexuality diet is based on the principle that food is not a substitute for sex but its enthusiastic consort; that a healthy body is a happy and energetic one; that there is more to life than slim hips and a good complexion (or, as your mother might point out, there is no use in buying a car if you don't intend to use it), and that we all know what the best exercise is.

The first thing to understand is that diet here does not mean slimming but, as originally intended, a way of life. Many of the recipes and suggestions in the book are, in fact, exuberantly uncalorie-conscious and flagrantly self-indulgent, and might even be considered fattening if they didn't so effortlessly lead to the perfect way to burn off calories and excess weight. Slimmers will, however, find that most of the recipes can be easily adapted or modified for calorie control, and that the foods highest in energy, vitamins and aphrodisiac qualities are often the natural slimmers as well.

The second thing to understand is that eating the right foods in the right amounts is only part of the regime. *The high-sexuality diet* not only includes an eye-opening (among other things) guide to aphrodisiacs, but sections on miracle foods, easy exercises to make you supple and relaxed, and an introduction to oriental dance and massage techniques to make you pleasantly aware of your body and to increase your own sensuality. It is, indeed, a total approach and one that will not only show results in better skin, hair, muscle tone and increased vitality (and an increased flow of all those vital juices), but one that is fun – fun for you and for the man you choose to share it with.

So, off you go. Dim the lights, put something moody and romantic on the record player, decorate the table with flowers (don't forget, they do have a language of their own) and candles, take the phone off the hook (there is no point in having a conversation with your mother about the new rug she bought for the hall half-way through the Spaghetti à la Don Juan and the detailed description of your belly dancing), and start to discover a new, prettier and happier you.

As Mae West might have said: you've only got one life to live, so you might as well live it.

1. The secrets of aphrodisiacs

Aphrodisiacs have been used for centuries to cure impotency, stimulate desire, inspire love and woo the reluctant lover when all else has failed. The ancient Egyptians, Greeks, Romans and Chinese, for example, all knew and used a great number of aphrodisiacs, many of which are included in their writings on herbal remedies. Luckily for us, many of these have made it into the twentieth century, where, lo and behold, they are not only attracting new interest but are receiving scientific vindication. Recent studies now reveal that many traditional aphrodisiacs contain concentrated nutrients that stimulate and revitalize cells and improve the body's balance and functioning.

No longer can sexual myths and magic be dismissed lightly, especially with our increased awareness and interest in natural foods and the healing and beneficial qualities of herbs. Ginseng, for instance, first mentioned and very highly thought of in the Chinese pharmacopoeia, the Pen-ts'ao (or Herbal), which was written over 2000 years ago, is now enjoying a new resurgence of both popularity and respect. What then, I wonder, about the love potion revealed in an Egyptian papyrus of an infusion of liquorice root, honey, sesame seeds and fennel seeds, to be taken by the light of the full moon? And where did William Shakespeare learn about squeezing the juice of a pansy into the eyes of an unsuspecting sleeper, to make her fall in love with the first person she sees on awaking, as happens to Titania in 'A Midsummer Night's Dream'? In any event, recent research has certainly proved the value of much folk medicine, including so-called aphrodisiacs, which contain large amounts of nutrients and thus act as stimulants and energizers.

Many of the herbs, roots and vegetables used in the past were also linked with general rejuvenation. Today these natural beautifiers, such as honey and coconut oil, are used in cosmetics and various beauty products because they are not harmful (as chemical compounds can be) and because they work. Other plants became associated with sexual potency and/or performance because of their distinctive shapes, which were thought to be nature's way of indicating their medicinal value. Thus the long history and popularity of ginseng which so resembles the human form that a perfect male-shaped root would even be worn as a sexual amulet.

Let us not forget, however, that the name 'aphrodisiac' comes from Aphrodite, the goddess of love who sprang from the sea, and in doing so bestowed her special powers on fish and other seafood. Oysters, of course, have always been famous for a lot more than pearls. Though there is the story of the man who, told that eating a dozen oysters would increase his potency and sexual drive, immediately rushed out and did just that. Asked if they'd succeeded he shrugged his shoulders philosophically. 'Not really,' he replied. 'I ate a dozen, but only ten of them worked.'

Other traditional aphrodisiacs – such as powdered rhinoceros horn or a mixture of honey and frog's saliva – no longer have the appeal they once had, nor, one assumes, the availability. Even the most desperate lover would have to be drunk on more than love to try to acquire one of those. And under no circumstances should one consider Spanish Fly, perhaps one of the most notorious aphrodisiacs of them all, which inflames and irritates the tissues of the body and the genitals, causing acute pain and even death. One of the mistresses of the Marquis de Sade, as though she hadn't had enough to contend with, died horribly after a dose of Spanish Fly.

Fortunately for you and me, many, if not most, aphrodisiacs are very kindly provided by nature in the form of simple vegetables and herbs. Even something as common and unspectacular as celery contains enough male hormones for a dozen lost weekends. Exactly the same hormones, in fact, as the more luxurious truffle and more exotic caviar. The list of aphrodisiacs which follows not only features those of historical renown but those that are nutritionally valuable as well. So whether you use them as a love potion or a tonic, you are certain to win.

The main aphrodisiacs

Asparagus
is rich in amino acids and minerals, especially potassium, phosphorus and calcium. These are necessary to maintain a high energy-level. Asparagus has gained a reputation as an aphrodisiac because it contains a diuretic which, when taken in large quantities, excites the urinary passages thus stimulating the genitals and causing an erection. Perhaps it is its shape that gives it its power – after all, the powers of suggestion on the subconscious are well known.

Caviar
the most blatantly indulgent of the aphrodisiacs, is valued as such largely because of its place in the reproductive process. The roe of mature female sturgeon, caviar is very high in protein. Just eating fresh caviar is in itself sensual: the taste is soft, rich and fleshy, and there is great pleasure in feeling the grains break in your mouth. Possibly Aphrodite gave the sturgeon that little bit more of her sensual powers. No wonder it's so expensive!

Celery

contains the same male hormones (pheromones) as truffle and so has the same aphrodisiac powers. It has the advantage of being far less expensive and is more easily available and is best taken as an infusion. Boil about a dozen fresh branches and leaves of celery in ½ pint of water for 30 minutes. It may not be the taste sensation of the year, but the effects are amazing.

Garlic

has been used as a medicinal herb by most of the great ancient civilizations. The Babylonians were using it in 3000 BC and both the Greeks and the Romans sang its praises as a tonic and an aphrodisiac. Roman soldiers were given garlic for strength and to sustain them on their long marches and even Hippocrates, the Father of Medicine, recommended it highly. The Egyptians too considered it a cure-all, a miracle herb and their pyramid builders consumed it for strength. But I prefer the use of garlic in folklore where it is considered a male aphrodisiac and is always planted next to roses to make them bloom.

Garlic is very nutritious, containing a large amount of vitamins B and C, and minerals, especially phosphorus, potassium and calcium, as well as some protein. But the vital ingredient in garlic is the volatile oil that produces its strong smell and its antiseptic properties. Garlic probably earned its reputation as a tonic and aphrodisiac because it exerts a remarkably warming effect on the body. It is also believed to prevent premature ageing and other ailments. Recent tests show that it can reduce high blood-pressure and the level of fat and cholesterol in the bloodstream. Taken daily with food, or as capsules, it is a valuable aid to good health and vitality – both necessary ingredients for a wonderful sex life.

Ginseng
has long been used in the East as a cure-all. The Chinese, who have been using it for more than 5000 years, consider it the best of the aphrodisiacs. Giving little thought to the saying 'never mix business with pleasure', they found that ginseng increased their sexual drive to such an extent that they could make love and take part in business discussions at the same time. Something to bear in mind when you next go to the office. The root resembles the human body, hence its name which means maman-root! It is believed that the more the root resembles a man's body the more fantastic the effects. The most efficacious is the red root which is therefore much more expensive than the yellow one.

Research into the properties of ginseng have shown it to contain vitamins, minerals, a volatile oil which acts as a stimulant on the nervous system, and complex steroids. The latter are believed to work with the body's hormone system and to support the body's natural gland function.

Ginseng can act both as a sedative or a stimulant, as the body seems to be able to adapt the plant to its own particular needs. This explains its myth as a cure-all and its use, not only to increase the sexual drive, but also as a tonic to build up general vitality and give greater resistance to stress and infections. Not surprisingly, the ancient Chinese called it 'the elixir of life'.

For best results, the whole root should be used to obtain all the properties in the right proportions.

Honey
thousands of years ago was used as a medicine and a general tonic. It has also been known to enhance desire and improve sexual capacity. The ancient Greeks called it 'the nectar of the gods'.

Because it is pre-digested by the bee, honey is absorbed quickly into the bloodstream and the body can use it immediately to increase vigour. The sugars are primary energy-givers, but it is also full of the nutrients necessary for good health. Its aphrodisiac qualities could come from the pollen it contains.

For any results, it should be taken regularly – at least 2 tablespoons 3 times a day. However, you can probably get equally good results simply by having your man call you 'honey' 3 times daily!

Oysters

are one of the most well-known aphrodisiacs. They have been vouched for by many of the famous lovers in history, including the prodigiously gifted Casanova who called them 'a spur to the spirit and to love'.

Oysters are very nutritious and certainly not fattening. So those of you who are worried about your waistlines but have always wanted to emulate Casanova – rejoice! Oysters are very low in calories: 1 medium-size oyster contains only 10 calories. Their fat content is only 2 per cent of their weight. They are also very easily digested and contain many nutrients, particularly zinc, a deficiency of which causes sexual problems, and vitamin E, the virility/fertility vitamin.

Peaches

for a long time have been known to provoke the sensual appetite. The tree was associated with the Goddess Venus and the fruit considered by the Chinese to symbolize the female genitalia, with its sweet juices as the effluvia of the vagina. Even today peaches are still associated with lust: a brothel is known as a peach-house and attractive girls are called peaches.

Pumpkin seeds

can help your love life. They are especially beneficial to the male reproductive organs as they contain large amounts of protein and oil, which keep the prostate glands healthy. They are also the best sources of zinc, which is commonly used in the treatment of prostate disorders – a major cause of impotence among middle-aged men.

Truffles
are rich in protein. Their aphrodisiac powers have been praised by many famous lovers – Casanova, Rabelais and the Marquis de Sade, to name but a few. But you would need more than a few slivers to achieve their results!

Truffles contain the male pheromones, and sexologists attribute their aphrodisiac virtues to these hormones which are identical to those contained in the male boar's saliva at the time of mating. Just as the sow digs wildly in the soil looking for these precious mushrooms, so she hunts for her male!

Vitamin E
is believed to do wonders for your sex life and to increase hormone production. It is popularly known as the virility vitamin since it was discovered that male animals, even rabbits – yes rabbits – became sterile through a lack of it. It is now recognized as an essential vitamin for the reproductive organs – it helps both male and female fertility as well as aiding the restoration of male potency. Good sources of vitamin E are cold-pressed vegetable oils, especially wheatgerm, sunflower seed, safflower and corn oils; seeds; nuts; wholegrain cereals and breads; eggs; lettuce and broccoli.

2. The miracle/beauty foods

What follows is a selection of the natural foods which can be a valuable supplement to your diet because of their high vitamin and mineral content. They are important for keeping the body in peak condition and in producing new cells, especially if you lead a hectic, stress-filled life. They are also, of course, extremely helpful when you are recovering from an illness as they encourage the body to rally its own resources to heal naturally. For these reasons they are often known as the 'miracle' foods.

Each of these little miracles has a specific use or function in body maintenance and good health – so some are more suitable for one thing and some for another, depending on the different balance of nutrients which they contain. However, because these nutrients are supplied in their natural forms they are easily and readily absorbed and used by the body. This means that they help put the body into its natural balance, leading not only to better health but better performance as well.

Miracle or no miracle, these foods will not work properly all by themselves. A handful of bean sprouts and two pieces of wholemeal toast in the morning are not going to improve anything if you spend the rest of the day eating chocolate bars and bags of artificially flavoured crisps. All the fibre in the world won't get that body in shape if the exercise you get is bending down to tie your shoes. Your diet must be well-balanced, with a variety of nutritious and natural foods rather than refined or convenience foods which have not only been stripped of their nutrients, but which may contain additives which are additionally dangerous. Plenty of fresh fruits and vegetables, fish and poultry – remember, too many carbohydrates or too much fat in the diet will upset its balance and nullify the beneficial effects of other foods.

One last point: when it comes to miracles, there is nothing as powerful or as sure-fire as the human mind. Your attitude and your mood will always determine the final results. So while you're dancing out your exercises in the morning to Mick Jagger singing 'Let's Spend the Night Together' and popping handfuls of soya bean sprouts into your smiling mouth, think happy, think healthy, and think about what you'll be wearing (or not be wearing, as the case may be) the next time you fix Chicken Unforgettable for two.

The main miracle foods

Brewer's yeast
is a nutritional yeast found in flake and powder form. Not to be confused with the yeast used for leavening, brewer's yeast is a raw, edible food supplement high in B vitamins and protein. Add it to all kinds of raw or cooked foods – even sprinkle it on your popcorn – though you should be warned that it has a strong flavour which may take some getting used to.

Cider vinegar
is a valuable food supplement, containing many vitamins and minerals. These are easily absorbed into the system, acting as a tonic and restoring health and vigour. Cider vinegar is especially good for those who want to slim. Dilute a tablespoonful in a large glass of water and drink it with your meals. It helps digestion, enabling the food to be broken down more efficiently in the body. It also helps eliminate any impurities in the body, helping you to a clear skin and shining hair.

Fibre

is a complex mixture of mostly indigestible plant substances, also known as roughage. It plays an important part in the diet, producing a more efficient digestive system as well as improving your body shape and skin. Fibreless diets are the cause of many disorders such as constipation, diverticulitis, varicose veins, haemorrhoids and obesity. Therefore, make sure you include plenty of high-fibre foods in your diet: wholewheat bread, bran, brown rice, root and green leafy vegetables, fruits and beans. These also contain many other nutrients good for health and beauty.

Kelp

is a large brown seaweed that is usually dried, ground and sprinkled on food to add vitamins, minerals and flavour. It is a good source of vitamins, iodine and amino-acids and is especially rich in minerals, which tone up the muscles, help with nervous tension and control obesity by counteracting lethargy. Kelp also keeps the reproductive organs healthy.

Lecithin

is a polyunsaturated fat essential for the assimilation of the fat-soluble vitamins A, D and K. Its ability to emulsify fats helps keep blood vessels free of fatty deposits that contribute to high blood pressure and heart disease. Lecithin is also a beauty food as it helps keep the skin clear and smooth. It is rich in phosphorus which activates enzymes and plays a part in breaking down carbohydrates and fats into energy. It is also a good source of the B vitamins choline and inositol, and vitamins A, D, E, F and K. In addition, it gives a helpful immunity against infections and viruses. It is found in soya beans, nuts, wholewheat cereals, egg yolks and liver. Lecithin can also be purchased in granules, liquid, powder, or tablet form. Use in moderation.

Molasses
is a by-product of sugar-cane. It is the syrup which remains after the sugar has been extracted from the sugar-cane juice. This thick syrup is full of valuable food elements and has a very high mineral content. The three particularly important minerals are iron (of which it is one of the highest sources), which provides the essential haemoglobin in the red blood corpuscles; calcium, which is needed for strong bones, teeth and nails; and potassium which, balanced with calcium, keeps the muscles toned and nerve tissues healthy. Molasses also contains most of the B complex vitamins and also protein. It can be used as a sweetener in foods instead of refined sugar. Try to avoid the sulphured types.

Nuts
provide the body with energy, protein and plenty of fibre. They are rich in the B complex vitamins and vitamin E. They contain polyunsaturated fatty acids and several minerals such as phosphorus, zinc, potassium and magnesium, which keep hair, nails and skin healthy. Almonds are particularly high in protein, brazil nuts in zinc, coconuts in fibre and hazelnuts in vitamin E.

Parsley
is one of the richest sources of vitamin C, the beauty vitamin, which helps prevent fatigue. Other good sources of vitamin C are bean sprouts, oranges, kiwi fruits, strawberries, papayas, mangoes, asparagus and green peppers.

Seeds
are packed with nutrients and fibre, and are a concentrated source of polyunsaturated fats, essential for energy; they are also excellent for healthy blood vessels and strong nerves. *Sunflower* seeds give you a healthy circulatory system and heart; they are rich in vitamin E (20 I.U.), potassium (a lack of which weakens muscles

and heart), niacin and thiamin. *Sesame* seeds contain iron, zinc, B vitamins, vitamin E and sesamol which have been claimed to slow the ageing process. They are also very rich in methionine and tryptophan, two amino-acids which do not exist in non-meat foods. By combining sesame seeds with vegetables, pulses, other seeds and nuts, you will provide your body with all the essential amino-acids.

Soya bean
a very rich source of protein since it contains all twenty-two amino-acids that make up protein. It is therefore an important food for vegetarians. It is also rich in lecithin, vitamins and minerals. Soya can now be found in many forms – as soya bean sprouts, soya oil, soya sauce, soya flour, soya milk and soya ice-cream. All are available in health food shops.

Sprouts
such as alfalfa, beans, lentils and mustard seeds, contain all the potential energy and food stored for the growing plant. They help to detoxify the system and clear out cellulite, as well as being vitality foods. Use them in salads or as a vegetable. Be really adventurous and try growing your own!

Vegetable seeds/oils
such as safflower, sunflower, corn and soya bean oils, contain the 'good fats' essential to good health. These are the polyunsaturated fats or essential fatty acids such as linoleic acid, which is necessary for your body's day-to-day functioning, beautiful skin and good healthy nerves. They are also natural diuretics. Do not cut down totally on fats but use them in moderation.

Water
is one of the most essential aids to health and beauty. It helps to preserve body shape and avoid cellulite deposits.

Plenty of water is necessary for complete elimination of waste products from the body; when these are not completely eliminated, they can build up in the connective tissues and result in unsightly lumps, particularly on thighs, hips and bottom. You need to drink about six glasses of water a day. If you can't bear it, try sparkling mineral water. There is nothing like bubbles to give you that delicious zing.

Whole grains
are very high in B complex vitamins which help metabolism. *Wholemeal bread* is unrefined and consists of 100 per cent of the wheat grain, and it has all the original wheatbran and wheatgerm and a fibre content of 9 per cent. *Wheatgerm* is the part of the wheat that germinates when the grain is planted and is therefore packed with nutrients. It is one of the best sources of B complex vitamins, vitamin E, iron and protein. It builds up energy stocks, helps fight fatigue and is excellent for the skin's beauty. Good sources are wholewheat bread, flour and cereals; or it can be bought as a separate product and added to food.

3. Beauty formulas

Probably when you were younger, and worried about spots or knobbly knees or the fact that your hair was not the colour of Mexican honey, your mother talked to you a lot about inner beauty. And probably you didn't really believe her. The truth, however, is that beauty really does start from within. Or, to re-coin a phrase that was fashionable a few years back, You Are What You Eat. To be seen at your best, to make the most of your own beauty and sensuality, however, you have to start with the basics – and the basics are the foods you eat. They – perhaps more than any other single factor – determine your mood, your energy, and the condition of every cell in your body from your toe-nails to your eyelashes.

Too many refined and processed foods in the diet (e.g. white bread, white sugar, tinned vegetables, etc.) can cause both weight and cellulite problems as your body takes longer to break them down and longer to get rid of the wastes. Additionally, they may contain chemicals or additives, as well as not containing the necessary nutrients. Poor nutrition makes the body an inefficient machine, drains energy and complicates its easy, natural functioning. How can you look your best if you never give yourself a chance to feel your best?

The best foods for keeping one in tip-top condition are, of course, the natural foods. These are foods such as whole grains, fruits and vegetables – either eaten raw or with a minimum of cooking and processing. Besides these, your body also needs its share of good protein to build cells, provide energy, and ensure muscle strength and tone. Demand nothing less than the very best – you deserve it.

The following list is designed to help you pinpoint your own problem areas and work to improve them, as well as building on your own obvious strengths.

The main beauty formulas

Hair

if not a woman's fortune, is certainly one of her greatest assets, and probably one of the first things a man notices about her. Indeed, men often remember the colour of a woman's hair much better than the colour of the dress she was wearing when he saw her from across the room, or the colour of her eyes as she flashed him her come-hither smile. A woman's hair – one might say – is the first thing he notices and the last thing he forgets. It is important, therefore, to take the best care of it possible. No destructive perms, dyes or bleaches; no tortured styles. And, most importantly, the right foods. Hair needs good protein (fish, lean meat and eggs), the B complex vitamins (wholegrain breads, cereals, legumes, dairy products, bananas, sprouts, leafy green vegetables, brewer's yeast, liver), and iron (red meat, liver, lentils, leafy green vegetables, molasses, legumes, wholegrains, almonds). If you have problems such as split-ends, brittle, dull, or dry hair, concentrate on incorporating the above foods into your diet and cutting down on salt, sugar and saturated fats. You should soon notice the difference.

Skin

reflects your inner chemistry. If you do not take enough fluids, especially water, your skin will be dry – and wrinkles show more on dry skin. Too many animal fats, sugar and fried foods in your diet will result in a greasy skin and spots. If your skin does not receive the proper nutrients, it is more likely to age prematurely so, to help keep your skin smooth and glowing, you should eat plenty of vegetables, especially watercress, spinach, cabbage, green peppers, spring onions and lettuce. These supply the vitamins A, E and K, which are all necessary to keep the skin healthy. Vitamin C is also useful as it maintains collagen, which aids the formation of connective tissues, keeps the skin firm yet elastic, and prevents wrinkles and stretch marks. The B complex vitamins are also necessary to keep skin youthful, since they control the skin secretions.

Eyes
if they truly reflect the soul, then you certainly don't want your eyes looking tired, lustreless and dull. And if you consider how many men have been seduced by a stranger's eyes (or even by a familiar pair of eyes) you will realize just how important a part they play in your love life. No matter how much you spend on mascara and eye liner, subtle eye shadows and globs of glitter, though, the only way to have bright, interesting-looking eyes with the attraction power of a magnet is to eat the right foods. Vitamin A (yes, from the reliable carrot, but also from tomatoes, eggs and liver, and green and yellow vegetables) will help strengthen your eyes and make them sparkle more than any expensive cosmetic ever could.

Nails
the long, boldly coloured nails of the old-time vamps are always alluring. But no one's nails – be they long or short – will lure anyone if they are chipped and broken. Wear your nails to suit your life-style (there is no point in trying for three-inch daggers painted blood-red if you are a joiner or a typist), but to keep them strong and beautiful you will need plenty of calcium, sulphur and phosphorus (milk, eggs, legumes – beans, lentils and peas – nuts, potatoes, greens and most fruits).

Stress

a certain amount of stress is actually good for you, helping your body to function better and meet extra demands. But too much stress over a long period of time (like too much champagne over too long a weekend) can ruin your looks and damage your health. Many skin and figure problems are caused by stress, and, because the nervous system is disturbed, you may also suffer from fatigue and irritability – not to mention a loss of interest in sex. The B complex vitamins, especially thiamine, and vitamin C are particularly important in combating stress. A sound diet, with plenty of fresh fruits and vegetables, will also help to increase your stress threshold.

Slimming

your body should always have enough exercise and proper nourishment. If you have a weight problem, fatty foods, sugars and heavy starchy foods that are difficult to digest are best avoided. Some nutrients help you achieve a good body contour and they should be part of your regular diet. *Iodine* helps in the smooth functioning of the thyroid gland, the weight regulator of the body. Good sources are seafoods and kelp. *Lecithin* helps you burn up fat deposits and is a natural diuretic, eliminating excess water from the body. Rich sources are nuts, seeds and lecithin granules. *Cellulite* is created by too much toxin in the body. The wastes are trapped in a mixture of fluid and fat, causing skin which is unattractive and resembles orange peel. Eat fresh and natural foods regularly, avoid canned and refined ones and increase your intake of fibre and water to flush out the system. Alfalfa sprouts, in particular, help to clean out tissue wastes. Blockages interfere with cellular metabolism and cause cellulite. Seafoods are also helpful as they contain iodine, known as the anti-cellulite mineral, which improves metabolism.

Vitality

you may not really be able to stay forever young, but having vitality will certainly keep you youthful and make your life more stimulating and exciting. Good nutrition, regular exercise and relaxation are the essential ingredients.

4. Beauty cocktails

These blender drinks are easy and quick to prepare. They supply your body with instant energy and are useful when you are in a hurry and have little time to sit down to a proper meal. They are highly nutritious and can also be used by slimmers as a meal replacement.

They contain plenty of the vitamins A and C which maintain healthy skin and hair; the B complex vitamins which help to fight stress and its effects on the nervous system; and minerals, especially calcium, which is necessary for strong, healthy nails and teeth. These drinks are therefore excellent for your looks as they contain the protein, vitamins and minerals necessary to maintain and preserve beauty.

The following cocktails are not only excellent for your looks, they are also high in energy. Save a teaspoon to give yourself a facial feast. It will improve your complexion and give a fresh glow to your skin.

High energy drink 1

½ lb small carrots, scraped and chopped
1 celery stick, chopped
1 small cucumber, sliced
1 small bunch parsley, chopped
salt to taste
juice of 1 lime
juice of 1 grapefruit

Put the vegetables in a blender, saving some cucumber slices for garnish, with the parsley and a little salt. Blend at high speed until the mixture is very smooth. Add lime

and grapefruit juices. Serve chilled with ice-cubes and decorate with cucumber slices.
140 calories, 30 carbohydrates

High energy drink 2

¼ pint natural yoghurt
¼ pint soya milk
4 oz wheatgerm
1 tablespoon sesame seeds
1 teaspoon honey

Blend all ingredients together. Sweeten with honey and serve.
200 calories, 28 carbohydrates

High energy drink 3

2 cups skimmed milk
2 raw eggs
1 ripe banana
1 teaspoon carob powder

Blend for a few seconds.
295 calories, 28 carbohydrates

High energy drink 4

2 cups skimmed milk
2 raw eggs
1 tablespoon brewer's yeast
1 tablespoon molasses

Blend together.
270 calories, 20 carbohydrates

These last two drinks are rich in B vitamins and are excellent in correcting mental depression, dry skin, dull complexion and lack of appetite.

5. The high-sexuality diet

Food does more than just nourish your body. In western culture, the body's breakdown and use of food is considered only as a physical process, but in the East it has long been thought of in emotional and spiritual terms as well. As my grandmother – who was something of a grass-roots philosopher – once put it, 'Animals feed, but people eat'. The quickest way to pep up your pleasures and spice your life is through your diet.

The high-sexuality diet consists primarily of high-energy, natural foods – with a generous additional helping of foods which are aphrodisiacs or especially sensuous and stimulating to more than one appetite. You wouldn't think of running from Cardiff to Oxford without the proper training – including the proper diet – so why should your life as a sexual being be treated any differently (or with any less thought and concern) than your life as an athlete? Besides, the chances are (with a little luck) that you're going to make love a lot more times than you're going to bike across Bristol or appear in the finals of 'Come Dancing', so why not take your sex life as seriously as you take the other parts of your life? Real results can be achieved, but only if you permanently change your diet and routine. Eating a piece of cod once a month is not going to improve your sex life, but making seafood an integral part of your diet probably will. Seafood contains most of the vitamins and minerals your body needs, as well as being traditional aphrodisiacs. Different varieties, of course, will also have their own special virtues: crabs and prawns, for instance, rich in phosphorus, aid the memory, while winkles, the richest source of magnesium, maintain youthfulness. In fact, scientific tests have proved that magnesium fights ageing, mental depression and fatigue. Seafood having little or no sugar and fat, are ideal for slimmers. Kelp and shellfish are especially important as they are rich in the minerals which fight obesity by stimulating activity.

Most of the other foods included in *The high-sexuality diet* (with the sensuous exception of a few titillating, indulgent and exotically stimulating recipes for very special occasions) also contain minimal amounts of fat, so you should be able to keep quite trim without having to try too hard. Liver and game, for instance, are much less fattening than red meats, and chicken and game (especially partridges) are believed to be good aphrodisiacs for men. The vegetables included in the diet are especially good sources of vitamin E – the precursor of silicone and sex hormones – which helps keep the skin smooth and flowing, and fights over-enthusiastic ageing.

Unsaturated fats are necessary to the body, but should be consumed in small and limited amounts, either as plant or seed oils (e.g. corn, sunflower or peanut, etc.), or the actual seeds or nuts themselves. Use a tablespoon or two in cooking or in salads. The fat in your meals also helps with the absorption of the fat-soluble vitamins A, D, E and K.

The high-sexuality diet is also high in fibre foods like wholemeal bread, potatoes, brown rice, fresh vegetables and fruit juices, all of which contribute to providing the body with the essential roughage it needs for proper digestion and to keep the body running smoothly and to strengthen resistance against disease. With your body ticking along as it was meant to, you are bound to be filled with the old *joie de vivre*, youthful vitality, and a healthy interest in the sort of non-aerobic exercise that requires two participants. If you have never understood what people mean when they describe someone as having 'the smile of the day after', this is your perfect opportunity to find out.

The high-sexuality diet is fundamentally a high-energy diet, designed to give you both energy and enthusiasm in abundance. Especially with the sort of lives we tend to lead today – demanding, hectic and requiring endless stamina – and with the popularity of leisure-time exercise it is important to take care of your body and ensure that it is receiving the right nourishment for the performance you expect from it.

Everything you eat provides energy, but to increase your stamina and stress-capacity, you should eat good quality foods, minimally processed (if at all) and containing maximum nutrient value. Wholewheat breads and cereals, wheatgerm (particularly useful in building up energy stocks and in fighting fatigue), honey, and seeds and nuts (the perfect natural snack foods), for instance, provide your body with proteins, vitamins, minerals, fibre and essential fats, and should be part of your daily diet.

Each meal you eat should contain a balanced and varied complement of foods. Breakfast is especially important (just as your mother always told you it was) because it establishes your basic energy for the day. If you have time, you should sit down to a proper cooked breakfast of eggs, toasted wholemeal bread, fruit juice and a piece of fresh fruit, but if, like many of us, you are usually late or about to be late and in a hurry to start running for your bus, then blender drinks or muesli are ideal. Quick to make, quick to eat, and endlessly variable, they give you the nutritive punch you need to get off to an energetic start. Lunches and dinners should contain one of the following: fish or shellfish, poultry, liver, steak, game, eggs, or cheese. All of these foods are high in protein – necessary for building and repairing body tissues – and minerals. Wholegrain breads, root vegetables, brown rice and wholewheat pasta all provide the fibre and carbohydrates needed for a healthy digestive system and the energy for muscular work. Plenty of fruits and vegetables (especially raw) are also essential to your health and vitality. If you have always been the sort of person who thinks of vegetables as a spoonful or two of tinned peas dumped between your meat and potatoes for a bit of colour, it is time you changed your ways. Have you ever heard of a fattening vegetable? The much maligned potato, an extremely important food of roughly the same caloric value as an apple, is not fattening, it is the butter and gravy in which we drown it that is to blame. Dress your salads and vegetables with lemon juice and fresh herbs and you will not only soon lose your taste for beans on toast and mushy peas, but be able to eat as much as you like without worrying about putting on weight.

As well as eating, naturally, a person must drink. Your drinks should mainly consist of fruit or vegetable juices, skimmed or soya milk, water and herbal teas. Alcohol is best left for special occasions, but if you like a glass of wine with your meals make sure that it is only one or two as too much will decrease your energy and ruin your other appetites.

The absolute no-no foods, leading to lethargy and fatigue, are: starchy, refined foods such as white flour, white bread and white sugar, canned and processed foods containing unattractive additives like sugar, colouring agents, starch and preservatives. You should also cut down on saturated fats, butter and margarines, cakes, pastries, chocolate, tea and coffee (except decaffeinated coffee and herbal teas).

Below is a basic outline of the foods – and their amounts – that should become part of your daily diet:

* Eat fish/seafoods 3–4 times a week.
* Eat liver or game once a week.
* Eat at least 1 of the following every day: asparagus, broccoli, cauliflower, carrots, celery, cucumbers, mushrooms, onions, radishes, truffles, spinach, watercress, tomatoes or peppers.
* Eat 2 raw green salads a day.
* Have 1–2 tablespoons unsaturated salad oil a day.

* Twice a week eat a side dish of lentils or soya beans.
* Eat at least 1 serving of wholemeal bread or potatoes or brown rice a day.
* Drink or eat 2 tablespoons of honey, wheatgerm or brewer's yeast, in fruit juices, warm water, cereals or meals every day.
* Drink fresh vegetable juice and/or fruit juice (with pulp) at least 3 times a day.
* Eat fresh fruit 2–3 times a day (especially peaches, oranges and bananas).
* Drink 2 glasses of skimmed milk a day.
* Drink at least 6 glasses of water/mineral water a day.

You can further enrich the sensual element in your diet by including plenty of ginger root, garlic, ginseng, parsley, pumpkin and sunflower seeds, bean sprouts, dill, cinnamon, marjoram, rosemary, basil, lemon and lime. Cayenne, black pepper, paprika, chillies and curry spices are also supposed to increase sexual vitality. This is possible because, when they are digested and passed into the intestines, they provoke a small dilation of the blood vessels in the lower abdominal area, stimulating the genitals. But you must be careful of the amount you use, as too much may ruin your food even as it sets you alight.

The recipes that you will find on the following pages are meant to suggest the sorts of things you can do to urge on your own creative and sensual potential. Although most of them are made for two, they can be easily adapted for more or less if you wish to practise (though I am certainly not suggesting that you hold an orgy – who in their right mind would want to join a conga line when there's a chance to dance to a waltz?).

6. Switch–on breakfasts

These are devised to give you a bright start to the day. From blender breakfasts, to sensuously sophisticated ones, there is something for you here, whether you need to whip up enthusiasm and energy for that morning 'after' or just to enjoy the day in bed with that special person!

Whip-ups for quick revival

* Pour into a blender, 2 cups of milk, 2 dessertspoons bran, 1 tablespoon lecithin granules, 2 raw eggs, 1 banana and a few ice-cubes. Blend for 30 seconds until light and frothy.

* Blend for a few seconds, 1 pint milk, 1 egg, 1 teaspoon honey and 1 tablespoon of brewer's yeast.

* Blend together, ½ pint fresh orange juice, 1 egg, 1 tablespoon lecithin granules and 1 teaspoon honey.

Muesli concoctions

* 4 tablespoons of rolled oats mixed with 1 segmented orange, 2 kiwi fruits, 2 oz mixed nuts, 1 tablespoon of sunflower seeds and 1 tablespoon of honey. Serve with milk.

* Bowl of bran, add sliced bananas, chopped hazelnuts and cashews, sultanas and milk.

* 4 tablespoons of millet, add 3 thin slices of ginger, a few chopped dates, sesame seeds, raisins and hulled pumpkin seeds. Sweeten with honey and serve with milk.

You can vary with buttermilk, soya or goat's milk. Endless combinations can also be made by using a selection of nuts and fruit, such as fresh or dried prunes, apricots, figs, apples, etc. Nuts are easier to digest when eaten with fruit.

Potent brunch

* Fresh oysters arranged in a pyramid and garnished with lemon slices. (Although Casanova ate fifty oysters for his breakfast; you may start with only a dozen each!)

* Caviar served on toasted French bread with a squeeze of lemon juice.

* Smoked eels with rye bread and a dash of fresh lime juice.

* Sea-urchin roe eaten raw on crackers; or fried in a little oil with freshly chopped chives and a sprinkle of lemon juice; or steamed and cradled in mussel, scallop or clam shells. This beautiful orange roe, shaped like a five-pointed star, can rival the finest caviar.

For total euphoria, serve brunch with champagne and fresh fruit – wild strawberries, pineapples, mangoes or melon.

7. Hot soups

If you need a little help getting the temperature to rise. . . .

These are excellent for warming and spicing up relationships. Some, like Lobster Bisque and the Bouillons, can be served as an entrée; others, like the Onion and Potato Soup, Pigeon Soup, and Beef with Lovage Soup, can be a meal in themselves. Even more exciting is the Golden Mulligatawny which can be eaten before, during or after the meal.

Consommé Rasputin
Some people call it madness . . . and some people call it love.

- 1 wild pigeon
- 1 small onion, peeled, leave whole
- 1 tomato, chopped
- 1 carrot, sliced
- 1 oz tomato juice
- 2 bay leaves
- ½ stick cinnamon
- 2 whole cloves
- ½ teaspoon whole peppercorns
- salt to taste
- 2 pints water

Put all the ingredients in a saucepan, add water, cover and simmer gently for 3 hours. Remove the bird (it can be served cold with a green salad). Strain and leave the liquid to cool. Skim off the fat and re-heat before serving.

Soup of beef with lovage

The perfect dish to warm up those long, cold nights. . . .

1 lb shin of beef, cut into large
  pieces
a few peppercorns and juniper
  berries
2 small onions
1 carrot, halved
2 tomatoes, chopped
2 heaped tablespoons dry
  mushrooms

4 sprigs thyme
6 sprigs fresh lovage
1 small piece ginger root,
  thinly sliced
salt to taste
4 sprigs parsley, finely
  chopped

Place the shin of beef in a saucepan with peppercorns and juniper berries. Cover with cold water and bring slowly to the boil. Then skim off the froth on the surface. Add onions, carrot, tomatoes, mushrooms, thyme and lovage. Cover and simmer for about 2 hours. 15 minutes before end of cooking, add ginger slices and salt. Sprinkle with parsley before serving.

Wonder broth

Wonder no more. . . .

1 large marrow bone (ask the
  butcher to cut it into 3–4
  pieces)
2–2½ pints water
1 teacup dark lentils, soaked
  overnight
1 large carrot, halved
2 sticks celery, halved
2 slices pumpkin, peeled and
  cubed

1 large onion, peeled and
  halved
1 teaspoon whole black
  peppercorns
2 sprigs thyme
salt to taste
4 sprigs parsley, finely
  chopped
2 bay leaves

Put the marrow bone pieces in a large saucepan with the water and bring to the boil. Skim off the froth which will have risen to the top. Then add the lentils, carrot, celery, pumpkin and onion. Season with pepper, bay leaves and thyme. Cover and simmer for 1½ hours. Add salt 30 minutes before end of cooking. Before serving the soup, remove the bones and sprinkle with parsley. Serve the marrow from the bones on baked potatoes with a generous sprinkling of ground black pepper.

Tender-pigeon soup

To keep him warm and cosy in your own special love-nest.

- 2 tablespoons olive oil
- 1 young pigeon, cut into pieces
- 1 teaspoon crushed ginger
- 1 clove garlic, crushed
- 2 sprigs fresh thyme or ½ teaspoon dried thyme
- 2 small tomatoes, chopped
- 1 teaspoon whole black peppercorns
- 1 pint water
- 4 oz vermicelli
- salt to taste
- 1 tablespoon chopped spring onions

Heat the oil in a saucepan and sauté the pieces of pigeon with ginger, garlic and thyme. Add tomatoes, peppercorns and water; cover and simmer for 45 minutes. Add vermicelli and cook till tender. Season with salt and sprinkle with spring onions before serving.

Onion and potato soup

Great chefs and great lovers all know the secret of bringing out the spectacular and the special in the ordinary. . . .

- 2 large potatoes, peeled and chopped
- 2 large onions, peeled and chopped
- 3 tablespoons sunflower oil
- 2 slices wholemeal bread, cut into cubes
- 1 clove garlic, finely chopped
- 1 pint water
- salt and freshly ground black pepper to taste

½ teaspoon paprika
2 tablespoons chopped fresh parsley
2 tablespoons grated cheese

Boil the potatoes in a little water until soft. Drain, then mash them with a fork. Fry the onions in oil, remove them and add to potatoes. Next fry the bread cubes with garlic and set aside. Add water to the potatoes, bring to the boil and simmer for about 10 minutes. Season with salt, black pepper and paprika. Serve with the cubes of bread floating in the soup, sprinkled with parsley and cheese.

Golden mulligatawny

A lovely hot dish with a heart of gold – sound like anyone you know?

2 small onions, chopped
2 tablespoons sunflower oil
4 tomatoes, chopped
1½ pints chicken broth, either stock or made with bouillon cubes
1 cup yellow split peas, soaked overnight
1 teaspoon tamarind pulp
salt and ground black pepper to taste

Mix together in a little water:
1 teaspoon crushed ginger root
1 clove garlic, crushed
1 tablespoon ground saffron
½ teaspoon ground aniseed
a few fresh coriander leaves

Stir-fry the onions in the oil until golden, add the spice mixture and cook for a few seconds. Add the tomatoes, chicken bouillon and yellow split peas. Cover and simmer for about 1 hour. Just before the end of cooking, add tamarind pulp and season with salt and black pepper.

Spicy red lentil soup

Lentils are one of the oldest known and most nutritious legumes; the seed is about 25 per cent protein which provides energy in abundance.

- 1 cup red lentils
- 1 pint beef broth, either stock or made with bouillon cubes
- 1 clove garlic, crushed
- 2 tomatoes, chopped
- 1 onion, peeled and sliced
- 2 tablespoons safflower oil
- 1 teaspoon ground saffron
- pinch grated nutmeg
- 2 cloves
- 2 sprigs thyme
- 2 bay leaves
- salt and ground black pepper to taste
- pinch paprika
- 1 tablespoon chopped fresh coriander leaves

Wash the lentils several times in cold water, put in a saucepan with the beef bouillon and bring to the boil. Meanwhile, stir-fry the garlic, tomato and onion in oil, then add to the soup. Lower the heat, add the spices, thyme and bay leaves. Cover and simmer for about 30 minutes. Season with salt, pepper and paprika and cook for about 15 minutes longer, until the lentils are soft. Sprinkle with coriander leaves and serve very hot.

Hot and sour soup

In China, bamboo shoots are believed to have aphrodisiac qualities, which accounts for at least some of their popularity. Give him a taste of the exotic East and find out for yourself. . . .

- ¾ pint fish or chicken stock
- 3 thin slices ginger root
- 1 cup bamboo shoots, sliced into matchstick pieces
- 8 Chinese dried mushrooms, soaked in warm water for 15 minutes, removed and sliced
- 1 teaspoon soya sauce
- ½ teaspoon tabasco
- 1 small glass rice vinegar (approximately 1 oz)
- salt and freshly ground pepper to taste
- 1 egg, well-beaten
- 1 tablespoon chopped fresh coriander leaves
- 1 tablespoon sesame oil

Place the fish stock with the ginger, bamboo shoots and mushrooms in a saucepan, bring slowly to the boil. Simmer for about 20 minutes, then add the soya sauce, tabasco, vinegar, salt and black pepper. Remove the saucepan from the heat and pour the beaten egg in slowly, stirring constantly. Add the oil and coriander leaves and serve immediately.

Tender hearts

He already knows you are bright, energetic and fond of exercise, now show him there's another side to you as well. . . .

2 small onions, peeled and sliced
a few sprigs fresh thyme
1 tablespoon olive oil
¾ pint water
6 pumpkin hearts† (young pumpkin shoots with tender leaves), chopped
1 cup bean sprouts
salt and ground black pepper to taste
1 tablespoon chopped fresh parsley

Stir-fry the onions and thyme in olive oil. Pour in the water and bring to the boil. Add pumpkin hearts and bean sprouts. Cover and simmer for about 15 minutes. Season with salt and black pepper, sprinkle with parsley and serve.

† As pumpkin hearts are a bit difficult to find in Britain, unless you grow your own, you can substitute a favourite green (like ½ lb Chinese cabbage leaves or turnip greens, or ¾ lb spinach).

Spectacular bouillon

Remember how your mother used to beg you to eat your spinach? Both spinach and watercress are very rich in vitamins C and E, as well as minerals which give you that special boost.

- 1 teaspoon crushed ginger
- 1 small onion, peeled and sliced
- 1 tablespoon chopped spring onions
- 1 tablespoon safflower oil
- 1½ pints water
- 1 small bunch watercress, remove coarse stalks, cut into small branches
- 1 lb spinach, coarsely chopped
- a few Chinese cabbage leaves, shredded
- 1 teaspoon soya sauce
- salt to taste

Stir-fry the ginger, onion and spring onions in safflower oil. Add water, bring to the boil. Add the greens, cover and cook for about 10 minutes. Stir in soya sauce and salt. Serve hot.

Smooth carrot soup

For extra insight into his intentions – and into yours. . . .

- ½ pint chicken broth, either stock or made from bouillon cubes
- 1 lb carrots, sliced
- 1 small onion, peeled and chopped
- salt and ground black pepper to taste
- 1 tablespoon finely chopped fresh parsley

Bring the chicken broth to the boil, add carrots and onion. Cover and simmer until the carrots are cooked – about 15 minutes. Season with salt and pepper. Purée, sprinkle with parsley and serve.

Wild mushroom soup

Bring out a little wildness of your own. . . .

1 lb wild mushrooms, cleaned and chopped
2 shallots, chopped
2 cloves garlic, crushed
2 cups water
salt and ground black pepper to taste
1 small glass milk

Place the mushrooms, shallots and garlic in a saucepan with 1 cup of water. Cover and simmer for 15 minutes. Season with salt and pepper, place in blender with milk and purée. Add the remaining cup of water and heat through.

Cinderella's soup

Serve to your prince in a hollowed-out pumpkin.

1 small onion, peeled and chopped
1 tablespoon sunflower oil
1 lb pumpkin, peeled and chopped into small chunks
1 wineglass apple juice
½ pint water
1 oz milk
pinch ground cinnamon
1 teaspoon marjoram
salt to taste

Stir-fry the onions in oil until soft. Add the pumpkin, apple juice and water. Cook until soft, add milk and blend. Reheat. Sprinkle with cinnamon and marjoram, salt to taste, and serve very hot (preferably before leaving for the ball).

Gorgeous black mussel soup

For something a little different. . . .

1 teaspoon crushed ginger root
2 cloves garlic, crushed
1 red chilli pepper, halved lengthwise
¼ lb mushrooms, cleaned, unpeeled
1 tablespoon olive oil
2 pints mussels, scrubbed and washed

2 tomatoes, chopped
1 oz white wine
4 sprigs thyme
¾ pint water

sea-salt to taste
1 teaspoon whole black peppercorns
croûtons

Stir-fry the ginger, garlic, chilli and mushrooms in olive oil. Add mussels and tomatoes. Stir for a few seconds, then pour the wine over. Add thyme, water, salt and pepper. Cover and simmer for 30 minutes. Serve with *croûtons* (small cubes of fried bread).

Aphrodite's bouillon

You might call this a gift from a goddess. . . .

4–6 small crabs
2 sprigs fresh thyme, or ½ teaspoon dried
1 teaspoon crushed ginger root
1 onion, peeled and sliced
1 tablespoon olive oil

4 tomatoes, chopped
1 pint water
1 teaspoon paprika
sea-salt to taste
juice of 1 lemon
1 tablespoon chopped spring onions

Wash and scrub the crabs, remove and discard the back shells. Quick-fry the ginger and onion in olive oil. Add the crabs and thyme and stir for a few minutes. Pour in the tomatoes, water, paprika and sea-salt. Cover and simmer for 30 minutes. Add lemon juice and spring onions. Serve hot.

Temptress bisque

This should certainly cause a rise in passion as all the ingredients are potent aphrodisiacs.

1 medium-sized hen lobster, boiled
1 teaspoon crushed ginger root

1 shallot, sliced
1 red chilli pepper, halved
1 tablespoon olive oil
1 tomato, chopped

2 sprigs thyme
½ teaspoon sea-salt
¾ pint water

1 tablespoon chopped fresh parsley

Cut the lobster in half. Remove the flesh and use it in the Island Salad (p. 54). Remove the claws, tail and the red-yellowish coral, and keep aside. Discard the hard shell. Quick-fry the ginger, shallot, and chilli in olive oil. Add the tomato and the lobster's claws and tail; stir continuously for a few seconds, then add thyme, sea-salt and the finely pounded red coral. Pour in the water, cover and simmer for 45 minutes. Strain the bisque, sprinkle with chopped parsley and serve hot.

8. Overtures

Hors-d'oeuvres, salads and chutneys à la fantasmagorique.

An overture is more than a beginning. It sets the mood, communicates your intentions and creates the right atmosphere of warmth and relaxation necessary for love. The recipes in this section are intended to arouse all of your appetites and to get your evening (or afternoon) off to the perfect start. Be daring. Be bold and adventurous. This is your chance not only to let him know what you are thinking, but to let him know what you are planning. So give your imagination free reign – be as suggestive and sinfully indulgent as you like. Just remember that the object is to titillate, not satiate. Fill him up now and he'll never make it through to dessert. And, of course, while you are whetting one appetite you should be stimulating others as well. Be careful, however, not to get too carried away before the main course – unless you are intending a truly unique hors-d'oeuvre. In which case, you should carefully plan the entrée so that it is something that can wait.

Hors-d'oeuvres

Venus shell

For the cook who knows exactly what she's starting. . . .

¼ lb mushrooms, thinly sliced
1 shallot, peeled and sliced
2 oz butter
1 small glass white wine
1 (7½ oz) tin red salmon, flaked
1 tablespoon milk
1 tablespoon double cream
sea-salt and ground black pepper to taste
1 tablespoon breadcrumbs
1 tablespoon chopped fresh parsley

Sauté the mushrooms and shallot in butter, pour in the wine and let it bubble for a few seconds. Then add salmon, milk and cream. Season with salt and pepper. When the mixture thickens, spoon it into empty scallop shells or ramekins. Sprinkle with breadcrumbs and parsley. Bake at 190°C (375°F, gas mark 5) for about 15 minutes.

Perk-you-up prawns

Prawns have a high content of phosphorus, which is involved in many bodily functions, sex being one of the more interesting of them. . . .

juice of 1 lemon
1 teaspoon cayenne pepper
10 large prawns, cleaned, shelled and halved lengthwise
salt and black pepper to taste
2 oz butter

Mix the lemon juice and cayenne pepper together. Arrange the prawns in an oven-proof dish and cover with the lemon juice mixture. Season with salt and pepper. Place a small knob of butter on each of the halved prawns and grill for about 5 minutes.

Canapés ronds aux crevettes

Delicate and deliciously different, each of these canapés could easily hold its own at a party or buffet – but they are also perfect for very special occasions.

6 slices French bread
butter
1 small cucumber, cut into slices

For the cocktail sauce, mix together:
2 tablespoons tomato sauce
1 teaspoon lemon juice
½ teaspoon finely chopped spring onions
Dash tabasco sauce
5 oz shelled prawns
2 tomatoes, sliced

Toast bread, then butter slices. Place one slice of cucumber on each piece of bread and fill the centre of each cucumber slice with cocktail sauce and prawns. Decorate with slices of tomato.

Canapés aux poissons

2 fillets of smoked trout
6 slices French bread
butter
2 tablespoons whipped cream
1 tablespoon grated cheese
pinch brown sugar
pinch of salt
1 teaspoon lemon juice
1 tablespoon chopped fennel leaves
6 lemon slices

Cut the smoked trout into small pieces. Toast the bread and butter it. Mix the cream with the cheese, add a pinch of sugar, salt and lemon juice. On each slice of bread, put a few pieces of trout and top with the cream and cheese mixture. Garnish with fennel and a slice of lemon.

Choufleur à la grecque

You don't always have to go away to discover vistas. . . .

1 cup water
1 oz white wine
½ teaspoon whole black peppercorns
½ teaspoon coriander seeds
2 sprigs thyme or ½ teaspoon dried
1 bay leaf
6 small onions, peeled
1 small cauliflower, cut into small florets
juice of ½ lemon
1 tablespoon olive oil
salt to taste

Pour the water and wine into a small saucepan; add peppercorns, coriander seeds, thyme and bay leaf. Bring to the boil. Add onions, cauliflower, lemon juice and olive oil. Season with salt, cover and simmer for about 10 minutes – the cauliflower should still be crisp. Allow to cool before serving.

Fiery avocado

Avocado has a high content of vitamin E, the virility vitamin. Whether your man is the type who needs a fire lit under him or not, this is just the dish to get things started. . . .

2 large avocados, peeled and diced
1 red pepper, seeded and sliced
1 teaspoon lemon juice
2 teaspoons soya sauce
½ teaspoon ground ginger
drop sunflower oil
1 teaspoon chilli sauce
pinch of salt and ground black pepper

Place avocado cubes and red pepper slices in a dish and sprinkle with lemon juice. Mix together soya sauce, ginger, oil, chilli sauce, salt and pepper. Pour over avocado and serve, preferably with a knowing smile.

Dream avocado

This avocado recipe is said to be more effective on women than on men. Potential Casanovas might use it to gain their lady's affections, but the really clever seductress will use it to improve both partners' moods.

2 large avocados, halved
2 tablespoons double cream
1 tablespoon lemon juice
a little chopped fresh basil or parsley

Remove the avocado pulp (do not damage the peel) and mix it with the cream and lemon juice. Sprinkle with basil. Serve in the avocado halves themselves.

Salads

Lover's salad

A garden of aphrodisiacs, this salad is good for everything – especially your sex drive.

1 lb tender spinach, roughly chopped
1 handful bean sprouts
3 tablespoons cress
1 tablespoon sunflower seeds
1 tablespoon pumpkin seeds (most important ingredient, should not be omitted)

For the dressing, mix together:
2 tablespoons sesame oil
1 teaspoon fresh lime juice (you can substitute lemon juice if limes are scarce, though you may want to add a little brown sugar or honey to the dressing as well)
2 tablespoons apple-cider vinegar
½ teaspoon sea-salt
½ teaspoon freshly ground black pepper

Wash and dry the spinach thoroughly, chill. Place the sprouts and seeds in a salad bowl, add spinach, pour dressing over, toss and serve.

Juicy melon salad

Melon and grapefruit particularly bring out the aphrodisiac qualities in cinnamon and nutmeg, as well as complementing each other's special taste.

1 honeydew melon
1 grapefruit, peeled and segmented
1 fennel bulb, sliced
salt to taste
pinch nutmeg
pinch cinnamon
1 teaspoon Worcestershire sauce

Cut the melon in half, discard seeds, remove flesh and cut into small pieces. Mix with the grapefruit segments and fennel. Season with salt, nutmeg, cinnamon and Worcestershire sauce. Serve the salad in the melon halves.

Surprise salad

Fennel, one of the ancient power herbs, gives this salad extra sexual potency. Just what the second surprise is depends on you. . . .

1 small cauliflower, outer leaves and coarse stalks removed	For the dressing, mix together:
	2 tablespoons yoghurt
	½ teaspoon mustard sauce
1 fennel bulb, chopped	1 tablespoon apple-cider vinegar
a few small pink radishes	pinch paprika
	salt to taste

Cut the cauliflower into small florets, place in a salad dish, add fennel and dressing. Toss well. Garnish with small pink radishes.

Sunkissed carrots

After serving this, it should be more than the carrots that are kissed. . . .

3–4 large carrots, grated	pinch of sugar
1 tablespoon raisins	salt and ground black pepper to taste
3 tomatoes, quartered	
1 tablespoon mint vinegar (vinegar flavoured with a little fresh mint)	1 teaspoon fresh basil or pinch dried basil
	2 kiwi fruits, peeled and sliced
1 teaspoon wheatgerm oil	

Put the carrots, raisins and tomatoes in a salad bowl. Season with vinegar, wheatgerm oil, sugar, salt, black pepper and basil. Decorate with slices of kiwi fruit and serve chilled.

Honeymoon salad

Both garlic and lettuce are aphrodisiacs. Lettuce can be given as an infusion to promote fertility or used as a mild sedative. I have named this salad after a very old joke, which is 'What's a honeymoon salad?' 'Lettuce alone'. The joke is feeble, but the salad is great.

1 lettuce, divided into single leaves	For the dressing, mix together:
6 black olives, stoned	1 clove garlic, finely crushed
	1 tablespoon sesame oil
	1 tablespoon mint vinegar
	salt and freshly ground black pepper to taste

Wash the lettuce leaves carefully several times. Drain and shake the leaves dry in a colander. Place in a salad bowl and toss well with the dressing. Decorate with black olives.

Suitor's salad

The potent ingredients in this salad almost guarantee that your suit will be successful. . . .

2 ripe avocados, peeled and sliced	For the dressing, mix together:
1 can (7½ oz) salmon, remove skin	1 tablespoon safflower oil
	2 tablespoons wine vinegar
1 small bunch watercress, stalks removed and cut into small sprigs	salt and ground black pepper to taste

Arrange on individual plates and cover with dressing.

Island salad

Imagine that you and your favourite man are stranded on a desert island with nothing to eat but the shellfish you catch yourselves and a few coconuts, and no one to talk to but each other and nothing to do but. . . .

1 medium-sized lobster, boiled
1 shallot, sliced
1 teaspoon fresh coriander leaves, chopped
1 teaspoon lemon juice
1 teaspoon olive oil
salt to taste
a few lemon slices

Remove the lobster meat from its shell, cut into thin slices and place in a salad dish. Mix well with the shallot, coriander leaves, lemon juice and oil. Season with salt. Decorate with lemon slices and serve.

Passion-hot chutneys

Love-apple chutney

This is very simple and quick to make, yet it is delicious. It liaises beautifully with any type of food – meat, fish, chicken, game or vegetables. Love-apple (pomme d'amour) is an old and infinitely more beautiful name for tomatoes – and also indicative of the powers with which that common fruit has always been credited.

6 tomatoes
1 onion, sliced
chilli sauce and salt to taste
2 tablespoons chopped spring onions

Grill the tomatoes. Allow to cool, then peel and mash with a fork in a dish. Add onion, chilli sauce and salt. Sprinkle with spring onions and serve.

Deceptive chutney

This is not just another shrimp chutney. Simple to make and delicious to eat, its secret ingredient makes it worth more than all the expensive perfume, dimmer switches and mood music in the world.

¼ lb shrimps
2 red chilli peppers, chopped
2 cloves garlic, chopped
1 small piece ginger root, chopped
3 ripe tomatoes, chopped

2 tablespoons olive oil
1 tablespoon garlic vinegar

Using a blender, mix the shrimps (including shells – which are especially important), chillies, garlic, ginger and tomatoes into a thick paste. Heat the oil in a pan; when hot, pour in the paste. Stir for a few seconds; remove from heat and add vinegar. Allow to cool before serving.

Stimulating sauce

There's more to life than stimulating the taste buds. . . .

- 1 teaspoon mustard oil
- 1 teaspoon sesame oil
- 1 tablespoon crushed ginger
- 1 teaspoon mustard seeds, crushed
- 1 small onion, peeled and finely chopped
- 1 oz ginseng wine
- 2 tablespoons apple-cider vinegar
- 1 teaspoon soya sauce

Mix the oils in a pan and heat. Add ginger, mustard seeds and onion. Stir for a few seconds then remove from heat. Mix with the wine, vinegar and soya sauce. This sauce is especially good with fish, pork or Tempura.

Angela's aubergine chutney

Angela – who was no angel – always swore that it was not her big blue eyes or lightning mind that attracted her many admirers, but this simple little recipe, learned on her travels.

- 3 aubergines, chopped
- 2 small onions, peeled and sliced
- 1 tablespoon mint vinegar
- 2 tablespoons natural yoghurt
- 2 tablespoons olive oil
- salt and ground black pepper to taste
- 1 tablespoon chopped fresh mint

Cook the aubergines in a little water until soft. Mash them with a fork. Add onions, vinegar, yoghurt and olive oil. Sprinkle with salt and pepper, mix well and garnish with mint. Serve with chicken and meat dishes.

Luscious lime chutney

The lime season is short in Britain, but this chutney makes it worthwhile to take advantage of it. Neither of you will be sorry.

4–6 limes
1 small piece ginger root, chopped
2 green chilli peppers, chopped
1 tablespoon olive oil
salt to taste

Place the limes in a jar, fill with salted water, cover tightly and leave to marinate for 3–5 days. Drain and chop the limes into small pieces. Blend into a thick paste with ginger, chillies, oil and salt.

Outrageous orange chutney

Oranges are also said to be aphrodisiacs. In Norfolk, the gift of an orange is supposed to win you the love of the recipient – though this recipe is so distinctive there's no telling what it will win you.

1 cup orange peel
1 teaspoon ground saffron
1 desertspoon mustard seeds
1 teaspoon chilli powder
salt and ground black pepper to taste
1 tablespoon olive oil

Place the orange peel in a small jar, fill with salted water, cover tightly and leave to marinate for 2–3 days. Drain, then cut the orange peel into small pieces. Place in a blender with the saffron, mustard seeds, chilli powder, salt, pepper and a little water. Blend into a thick paste. Heat the oil and pour it over the paste. Mix thoroughly and serve with one of the fish dishes for a really special sensation.

9. Lovable lunches

These are easy and quick to prepare, so you won't waste precious time in the kitchen. The Potted Shrimps and the Ox-Tongue in Aspic can even be prepared a day in advance so you will both have plenty of time beforehand to get into the mood for a romantic lunch, with perhaps pink champagne, or a bottle of rosé – and plenty of roses – and plenty of love!

Enchanting cloud omelette

Light as a kiss, subtle as a lover's smile. . . .

2 eggs	pinch *fines herbes*
2 tablespoons milk	salt to taste
1 oz black truffles, finely chopped	2 oz butter

Beat the eggs and milk lightly with a fork; add the truffles, *fines herbes* and salt. Melt the butter in an omelette pan; when foaming, pour in the mixture. With a wooden spatula, draw mixture from the sides to the middle of the pan, so allowing the uncooked egg to set quickly. Repeat until all the runny egg is lightly cooked. When the top is still slightly runny, fold over and serve.

Suggestion omelette

Just a little more bold and adventurous than your average omelette. It shouldn't take long for him to understand the suggestion. . . .

½ lb asparagus
4 eggs
2 tablespoons milk
salt and ground black pepper to taste
3 oz butter
1 tablespoon grated cheese (whatever kind catches your fancy)

Poach the asparagus briefly in a little water; it should remain crisp. Beat the eggs and milk together with a fork and sprinkle mixture with salt and pepper. Melt the butter in an omelette pan; when it starts sizzling, pour in the egg mixture. When the omelette is almost ready, lay the asparagus across one half of it, sprinkle with grated cheese, fold over and cook for a little longer.

Potent potted shrimps
What could be simpler . . . ?

¼ lb cooked shrimps, peeled
1 tablespoon cream
salt and ground black pepper to taste
butter

Pound the shrimps coarsely. Add the cream, salt and pepper. Pile into a small ramekin dish, seal with melted butter and store in the refrigerator. Serve with toast and slices of lemon.

Irresistible baked potatoes
You will never think of potatoes as ho-hum again.

2 large potatoes
4 tablespoons yoghurt
caviar

Scrub the potatoes and bake in their jackets until soft, about 1 hour, at 200°C (400°F, gas mark 6). When the potatoes are cooked, cut in half lengthwise and mash the soft centre gently with a fork. Place a tablespoon of yoghurt on each potato half and serve topped with a dollop of caviar. These should be accompanied with neat, chilled, clear Russian or Polish vodka, to make you even more irresistible to him and he to you.

Miracle mackerel with lime

If you don't believe in miracles you will now. . . .

- 2 mackerel fillets
- 2 small onions, peeled and sliced
- a few sprigs fresh mint, finely chopped
- 1 teaspoon fresh or bottled lime juice
- 1 green pepper, seeded and chopped
- sea-salt and freshly ground black pepper to taste
- 1 small lime, sliced (lemon can be substituted when limes are out of season)

Poach the fish in lightly salted water for about 6 minutes. Take out and cut into small pieces, removing any bones, and place in a dish with onions, mint, lime juice and green pepper. Sprinkle with salt and black pepper, mix well and garnish with slices of lime.

Scintillating sardines with love-apples

Whether you call them love-apples or tomatoes, their reputation it as well-deserved as yours will be. . . .

- 2 tins sardines, drained of oil and flaked
- 8 tomatoes, finely chopped
- 2 tablespoons chopped spring onions
- 2 small onions, peeled and sliced
- 1 teaspoon cayenne pepper

Mix all the ingredients together and serve with French bread.

Neptune's salad

Yet another treasure from the dark and wondrous sea. . . .

2 fish fillets (any white fish will do)
1 green and 1 red pepper, seeded and chopped
6–8 prawns, cooked and shelled
1 shallot, sliced
2 apples, seeded, cored and sliced
1 tablespoon chopped parsley
lettuce for garnish

For the dressing, mix together:
juice of ½ orange
a few drops of tabasco
1 teaspoon lemon juice

Poach the fish fillets for 15 minutes in salted water, and leave to cool. Then remove and cut fillets into small pieces: add peppers, prawns, shallot and apples. Add the dressing and mix well. Put the lettuce in a salad bowl, pour in the fish salad and garnish with parsley.

Ox-tongue in aspic

This is ideal for a picnic lunch, as the gelatine keeps the ox-tongue cool and moist, and leaves you time for warmer affairs.

(Prepare the dish a day in advance)

2½–3 lb ox-tongue
2 bay leaves
4 whole cloves
½ stick cinnamon
½ teaspoon whole black peppercorns
salt to taste
1 small carrot, halved across the width
1 packet gelatine

Place the ox-tongue in a large saucepan and cover with cold water. Bring very slowly to the boil, skimming frequently to clear the surface. Add bay leaves, cloves, cinnamon, peppercorns, salt and carrot. Cover and simmer for 3½ hours. Remove the ox-tongue and strain the liquid. Stir the gelatine into the liquid and replace the ox-tongue. Allow to cool, then leave in refrigerator to set. Serve with wholemeal bread and tomato chutney.

Grilled quails

Eating quails can be a highly erotic experience, so, although they are expensive, they are worth trying on at least one memorable occasion.

3–4 quails
2 tablespoons olive oil
salt and ground black pepper to taste
2 oz butter
1 teaspoon tarragon

Brush the quails with olive oil, sprinkle with salt and black pepper. Put a knob of butter, rolled in black pepper and tarragon, inside each bird, then place under a hot grill, turning from time to time, until golden brown. Serve with a green salad.

Bedside snacks

Some people do insist on having food in bed. It is difficult to understand why – but if you feel the need, these titbits will at least lead to other things. . . .

* Soft herring roes with watercress, lemon juice and a sprinkling of freshly ground black pepper.
* Salmon with sliced shallot, lemon juice and a sliver of truffle.
* Sardines with grated cheddar cheese, sliced onion and tomatoes and a sprinkling of paprika.
* Hard-boiled eggs with raw mushroom slices and anchovy fillets.
* Cottage cheese with cooked shelled prawns and a generous sprinkling of chives.
* Place a slice of smoked ham on a piece of bread; lay 6 cooked asparagus spears on top. Roll up another slice of smoked ham and place on the bed of asparagus.

Cuddly sandwiches

Special fillings for a special feeling. . . .

* Tuna fish with halved small white onions, crushed mustard seeds and nasturtium leaves.
* Ham slices spread thickly with horseradish and grated carrot.
* Grind sultanas, cashew nuts and almonds and mix with butter to make a paste. Use as a filling for sandwiches and sprinkle with fresh dates.
* Cottage cheese mixed with a crushed clove of garlic and finely chopped chives and marjoram.
* Banana, honey and milled brazil nuts mixed together.
* Put dried apricots through a grinder, add a tablespoon of cream cheese and milled nuts. Mix well and spread the paste thickly on each side of the sandwich.

10. Intimate dinners

No deep, meaningful relationship has ever been furthered over a bowl of tinned soup or a tuna fish sandwich, no matter what your friends may tell you. The recipes in this section – all, I might add, consumer-tested – have all been specially designed to bring you and the object of your affections closer together – in fact, as close as you can get. There is something for every taste from the man who only eats because he gets hungry to the most fanatical gourmet. After all, nothing tells a man your intentions more clearly the care, concern and thoughtfulness you show by serving him a special meal. Bang a plate of frankfurters and beans down on the table and the most ardent admirer is going to say to himself, 'You what?', and immediately begin remembering that woman he used to know who had such a wonderful way with a lamb stew. Show him you care with a special meal, a nice wine, and a few personal touches, and you may be surprised to discover just what he cares to show you.

Lobster in style
Something special for someone special. . . .

- 1 medium-sized lobster, boiled and halved
- 2 tablespoons sesame oil
- 2 shallots, chopped
- 2 small carrots, sliced thinly lengthwise
- 3 tablespoons champagne cognac
- 1 teaspoon cayenne pepper
- 2 tomatoes, chopped
- 1 teaspoon butter
- 1 tablespoon finely chopped fresh parsley

Remove the lobster's flesh from the shell and slice thinly.
Heat the oil in a pan; add shallots, carrots and lobster and
cook for a few seconds. Pour in the champagne cognac
and *flambé*. Then add cayenne pepper and tomatoes.
Cook for 8–10 minutes, add butter and serve in the shell
with a sprinkling of parsley.

Saucy but nice

*Hen-lobsters, because of the red coral inside, are believed to be
especially beneficial to the sex organs.*

1 hen-lobster, boiled
2 cups water
2 sprigs thyme
1 teaspoon cayenne pepper
2 cloves garlic, crushed
1 small onion, peeled and sliced
2 tablespoons olive oil
4 tomatoes, chopped

Cut the lobster in half, remove the flesh and red coral
(this gives the dish a most delicious flavour) and keep
aside. Remove the tail and claws of the lobster and pound
to a fine powder. Mix this with the water, add thyme and
cayenne pepper, and simmer for 15 minutes. Strain and
keep the juice. Stir-fry the garlic and onion in olive oil;
add tomatoes and cook until puréed. Then add lobster
meat, red coral and juice. Simmer for a further 10
minutes. Serve with boiled rice.

Understated grill

*You could almost call this the black dress of lobster recipes –
simple and easy, but sophisticated enough for the most sensitive
palate.*

1 medium-sized lobster
salt and ground black pepper to taste
1 oz butter

Cut the lobster in half lengthwise. Sprinkle with salt and
pepper. Place a knob of butter on each half and grill for
about 15 minutes.

Lobster in aubergines

This may not seem, at first glance, a good combination, but I can assure you that it is one of the most delicious lobster dishes I've ever tasted. Remember, that if you are adventurous in the kitchen, you probably are in bed as well. This is a good way to hint at the exciting things to come.

1 teaspoon crushed ginger
1 clove garlic, crushed
1 tablespoon olive oil
2 sprigs thyme or ½ teaspoon dried
1 medium-size lobster, boiled; remove flesh
½ lb aubergines, sliced
1 small glass water
2 tomatoes, chopped
salt to taste
1 tablespoon fresh chopped coriander leaves

Stir-fry the ginger and garlic in olive oil for a few seconds. Add thyme and lobster's meat. Cook briefly, stirring all the time. Add aubergines and water. Cover and cook on a moderate heat for 15 minutes. Add tomatoes, season with salt and cook for another 15 minutes. Sprinkle with coriander leaves and serve.

Prawn rougaille

An especially tasty Mauritian speciality, and one guaranteed to put you both in a relaxed and receptive frame of mind.

1 shallot, sliced
1 teaspoon crushed ginger root
2 tablespoons sesame oil
12 oz prawns, unshelled
1 oz white wine
6 tomatoes, chopped
2 sprigs thyme or ½ teaspoon dried
salt to taste
1 tablespoon freshly chopped chives

Stir-fry the shallot and ginger in the sesame oil for a few seconds. Stir in the prawns and pour in the wine. Add tomatoes, thyme and salt. Cover and simmer for 15 minutes. Sprinkle with chives before serving.

Sesame prawns

For the opening up of new doors. . . .

2 tablespoons sesame oil
¼ lb button mushrooms, chopped
12 oz prawns, shelled
2 tablespoons sesame seeds
salt to taste
1 tablespoon chopped fresh parsley
1 tablespoon lemon juice

Heat the sesame oil in a pan; sauté the mushrooms, then add the prawns, sesame seeds and salt. Cook for about 5 minutes, stirring continuously. Sprinkle with parsley and lemon juice.

Sweet-nothing prawns

The simplest temptations are always the best. . . .

12 oz prawns, shelled
3 oz butter
1 clove garlic, crushed
1 tablespoon chopped fresh parsley
salt to taste
2 tablespoons sherry

Sauté the prawns in butter, add garlic, parsley and salt. Stir, pour in the sherry, and serve immediately.

Persuasion mussels

Mussels are rich in magnesium which helps preserve youth and relaxes the nerves.

15–20 mussels, washed
2 tablespoons olive oil
2 cloves garlic, crushed
1 small onion, peeled and sliced
2 large red peppers, seeded and sliced
1 tablespoon chopped fresh chives

Boil the mussels in a little water until they open. Remove and discard the empty halves of the shells. Heat the olive oil in a pan, add the mussels, garlic, onion and red peppers. Cook for about 15 minutes, stirring all the time. Sprinkle with chives and serve.

Golden dream shrimps

With this sort of help you can easily make all your dreams come true. . . .

1 clove garlic, crushed	1 teaspoon red chilli sauce
1 shallot, chopped	½ teaspoon ground coriander seeds
2 tablespoons safflower oil	
½ lb shrimps, cleaned and shelled	4 tomatoes, chopped
	1 bay leaf
1 teaspoon ground saffron	1 oz white wine

Stir-fry the garlic and shallot in safflower oil. Add the shrimps, saffron, chilli sauce and coriander seeds. Stir for a few seconds then add tomatoes, bay leaf and wine. Simmer for 20 minutes. Sprinkle with chives and serve with rice.

Paradise crab

Crabs are eaten on tropical islands with lemon and onions; the islanders believe this combination to be a good sexual rejuvenant. And they are probably right.

2 medium-sized crabs, cleaned	1 tablespoon soya sauce
	juice of 1 lemon
2 large bunches spring onions, coarsely chopped	1 glass sherry
	a little sea-salt

Place the whole crabs in a large saucepan and cover with some of the spring onions. Mix the soya sauce, lemon juice and sherry together and pour over the crabs. Sprinkle with salt, cover tightly and steam on moderate heat for about 15 minutes. Serve on a bed of fresh spring onions.

Deep sea daube

Dried octopus is available in most Chinese supermarkets. Do not be put off by its appearance – which is less than beautiful – it is absolutely delicious. As well as being an incredible conversation starter.

- 2 tablespoons olive oil
- 1 teaspoon crushed ginger
- 1 clove garlic, crushed
- 1 small shallot, chopped
- 2 sprigs thyme and parsley
- 1 dried octopus, soaked for several hours in cold water, cut into small pieces
- 1 lb tomatoes, chopped
- 1 teaspoon cayenne pepper
- 1 small glass water
- salt and ground black pepper to taste
- 1 tablespoon chopped spring onions

Heat the olive oil in a pan; add the ginger, garlic, shallot, thyme and parsley. Stir for a few seconds, then add octopus pieces. Cook for about 5 minutes, then add tomatoes, cayenne pepper and water. Season with salt and black pepper. Cover and simmer for 1 hour. Sprinkle with spring onions just before serving.

Martin's marinated squid

Martin was one of the most handsome and charming men I have ever met, and a good cook, too. Not only did he have legendary success with women – but even ex-lovers had only good to say of him. Martin always claimed that this recipe was one of the secrets of his popularity. Could thousands of beautiful women be wrong?

- 1 lb fresh squid
- 1 cup vinegar
- 1 small glass white wine
- 1 teaspoon whole black peppercorns
- 1 bay leaf
- 1 small piece ginger root, thinly sliced
- ½ teaspoon sea-salt
- 2 tablespoons olive oil
- 1 tablespoon chopped fresh parsley.

Remove and discard the head, then clean the inside of the squid; wash well under running cold water, then cut into small rings. Leave to marinate for about 3 hours in the vinegar, wine, peppercorns, bay leaf, ginger and sea-salt. Then sauté in olive oil. Strain the marinade and add to squid. Cover and simmer for 45 minutes. Serve with a sprinkling of parsley.

Crafty carp in aspic

This should be prepared a day in advance, giving you plenty of time to prepare everything else.

- 1 carrot, sliced
- 1 shallot, sliced
- 2 sprigs thyme
- 1 bay leaf
- 2 cloves
- 6 whole black peppercorns
- 1 pint water
- salt to taste
- 1 medium-sized carp, cleaned and gutted
- 1 tablespoon lemon juice
- 1 oz gelatine
- a few slices lemon
- a few sprigs watercress

Place the carrots, shallot, thyme, bay leaf, cloves, lemon juice, peppercorns and salt in 1 pint of water and bring slowly to the boil. Place the fish (whole) in the bouillon and simmer for 12–15 minutes. Remove the pan from the heat; stir in the gelatine and allow to cool. Chill in refrigerator until set. Garnish with lemon slices and watercress sprigs.

Extravagant trout

The trick with most things, including seduction, is to take the ordinary and make it special. . . .

- 2 oz butter
- salt and ground black pepper to taste
- 2 tablespoons flaked almonds
- 2 medium-sized trout, cleaned and gutted
- juice of half a lemon
- a few sprigs parsley, trimmed
- a few lemon slices

Place a knob of butter rolled in pepper and almonds inside each trout. Pour the lemon juice over the trout: dot them with butter and sprinkle with the rest of the almonds. Place under a hot grill for about 5 minutes, then sprinkle with salt and grill for a further 15 minutes. The fish should remain pink inside. Garnish with parsley and lemon slices.

Tuna fish with tamarind

Once upon a time, tuna fish was what you ate when you were snowed in miles from nowhere and there was nothing else in the larder. Of course, once upon a time a nice girl would never think of seduction unless she was snowed in miles from nowhere.

1½ lb fresh tuna fish, cut into equal pieces
3 tablespoons olive oil
1 medium-size aubergine, diced
1 clove garlic, crushed
2 onions, chopped
2 tomatoes, chopped
2 bay leaves
salt to taste
1 tablespoon tamarind pulp
1 tablespoon fresh mint, chopped

Fry the fish pieces in olive oil, remove and keep aside. In the same pan, place the aubergine, garlic and onions and cook for about 10 minutes. Add the tomatoes, bay leaves, salt and tamarind pulp. Stir for a few seconds then add the fish. Cover and simmer for 45 minutes. Sprinkle with mint and serve with rice.

Elusive eel

Not perhaps, to everyone's taste – but then, what is?

6 ripe tomatoes, chopped
2 cloves garlic, crushed
1 shallot, sliced
2 sprigs thyme
2 rock eels, skinned and cut into equal-sized pieces
1 small glass port
1 tablespoon finely chopped parsley
salt and ground black pepper to taste

Cook the tomatoes, garlic, shallot and thyme on a low heat for about 10 minutes. Add the eels and port and cook for 15 minutes. Add salt and pepper to taste, sprinkle with parsley and serve.

Spring-love chicken

Once tasted, never forgotten. . . .

4 tablespoons olive oil
1 lb chicken joints
1 small glass apple-cider vinegar
1 small glass white wine
2–3 small potatoes, peeled
½ lb french beans, topped and tailed, chopped
1 teaspoon fresh basil
dash tabasco
salt and ground black pepper to taste
1 cucumber, diced
1 teaspoon capers

Heat the oil and sauté the chicken. Pour in the apple-cider vinegar and wine. Stir for a moment then add potatoes, french beans, basil and tabasco sauce. Sprinkle with salt and pepper; cover and cook on a moderate heat for about 25 minutes. Add cucumber and capers and cook for a further 10 minutes.

Chicken exotica

Chicken, like a good lover, is always adaptable. . . .

1 small pineapple, peeled, sliced into rings (or use tinned pineapple rings)
4 chicken breasts, boned and rolled
1 oz ginseng wine
juice of ½ lemon
salt to taste
1 teaspoon *fines herbes*

Make a bed of pineapple rings in an ovenproof dish. Lay the chicken rolls on top. Mix the ginseng wine and lemon juice together and pour over. Sprinkle with salt and *fines herbes*. Bake in a hot oven, 200°C (400°F, gas mark 6) for 35 minutes.

Chicken paprika
Originally from Hungary, where the nights are long, dark, cold and well-suited for intimacies, this is a dish for hearty lovers.

- 4 chicken drumsticks
- salt and paprika to taste
- 2 tablespoons sunflower oil
- 1 small onion, chopped
- 4 tomatoes, chopped
- 4 sticks celery, trimmed and chopped
- ½ teaspoon rosemary
- 1 glass chicken stock
- 1 tablespoon soured yoghurt (made by adding a drop of lemon juice to plain yoghurt) or soured cream
- 2 tablespoons chopped spring onions

Sprinkle the chicken with salt and paprika and fry in sunflower oil. Remove from pan and set aside. Fry the onions until soft, add tomatoes, celery, rosemary and chicken stock. Cover and simmer for about 20 minutes. Mix in the sour yoghurt and spring onions, stirring until the sauce is smooth. Pour over the drumsticks and serve with rice.

Haunting chicken
Just like you. . . .

- salt and ground black pepper to taste
- ½ teaspoon ground nutmeg
- 1 lb chicken joints
- 1 wineglass water
- 2 sticks celery, trimmed and chopped
- 1 small red pepper, seeded and chopped
- 8 cloves garlic, peeled
- 2 tablespoons brandy

Sprinkle salt, pepper and nutmeg on the chicken joints. Heat the oil in a casserole, add the celery and red pepper. Stir for a moment, then add the chicken and cook until browned on all sides. Add the garlic, brandy and water. Cover and cook in oven 220°C, (425°F, gas mark 7) for 1 hour. Serve with wholemeal bread.

Chicken unforgettable

Mushrooms and onions have rejuvenating properties and slow down the ageing process.

1 small chicken, cut into equal-sized pieces	1 onion, peeled and sliced
3 tablespoons olive oil	½ lb wild mushrooms, unpeeled and chopped
2 wineglasses white wine	1 tablespoon cream
salt and ground black pepper to taste	1 oz butter
1 tablespoon chopped fresh parsley	

Sauté the chicken pieces in olive oil. Add the wine, salt, pepper, parsley and onion. Cover and simmer for 45 minutes. Add mushrooms and cook for a further 10 minutes. Before serving, stir in the butter and cream.

Magic rabbit

If you set the stage correctly and let yourself get into the right sort of mood, this should lead to a much more interesting evening than watching bunnies pop out of hats.

2 lbs rabbits, cut into large pieces	1 onion, peeled and chopped
½ bottle red wine	4 tablespoons corn oil
1 small glass cider vinegar	2 sprigs thyme
1 teaspoon salt	2 bay leaves
2 whole cloves	1 teaspoon brown sugar
1 teaspoon whole black peppercorns	

Wash the rabbit pieces, put in a bowl with the wine, cidervinegar, salt, cloves and peppercorns. Place in the refrigerator and leave to marinate for 24 hours. Remove the rabbit pieces and pat dry with a paper towel. Brown them with the onion in corn oil. Strain the marinade and pour it into the pan. Add thyme, bay leaves and sugar. Cover and simmer for 1½ hours.

Pleasure partridges

The partridge has enjoyed its reputation as an aphrodisiac and a rejuvenant for many centuries. Its brain was powdered and mixed in red wine and its flesh, according to Platina, the historian, 'arouses half-extinct desire for venereal pleasures'. So start arousing. . . .

2 oz butter
salt and ground black pepper to taste
2 young partridges
1 small cabbage, shredded
½ lb mushrooms, finely sliced
1 small glass white wine
2 sprigs thyme

Roll the butter into small lumps. Cover in salt and black pepper, and put inside the birds. Place in a baking dish and roast inside a fairly hot oven at 190°C (375°F, gas mark 5). After 15 minutes, turn the birds over and baste with a little butter and the juices in the pan. Mix the cabbage and mushrooms together and put around the birds in the baking dish. Pour the wine over and sprinkle with salt, pepper and thyme. Return to the oven and cook for another 10 minutes. Turn the birds over again and mix the vegetables with the juices. The birds should be ready after another 10–15 minutes, and the cabbage and mushrooms should be deliciously flavoured with the juices from the birds.

Neither of the next two recipes could be considered everyday (or every night) fare. Reserve them for someone you really want to impress. Hare has an old and well-deserved reputation for exciting desire.

Roast saddle of hare

1 saddle of hare with hind legs, cut into large pieces
4 tablespoons olive oil
2 sprigs thyme
1 teaspoon chopped fresh tarragon

2 cloves
½ teaspoon ground cinnamon
pinch nutmeg
salt and ground black pepper to taste
1 small glass sherry
a few sprigs parsley

Baste the pieces of hare in olive oil and put them in an ovenproof dish. Add thyme, tarragon and cloves; sprinkle with cinnamon, nutmeg, salt and pepper. Bake in oven 190°C (375°F, gas mark 5) for 30 minutes, turning the meat pieces halfway through the cooking. Pour the sherry over and cook for another 10 minutes, garnish with parsley and serve.

Pheasant salmi

1 medium-sized pheasant, cut into large pieces
6 tablespoons olive oil
1 small onion, peeled and chopped
2 tomatoes, chopped
2 wineglasses red wine
juice of ½ lemon
1 cup chicken bouillon
2 bay leaves
1 teaspoon dried or fresh tarragon
½ stick cinnamon
4 cloves
salt to taste

Brown the pheasant in oil: add onion and tomatoes. Stir for a moment, add the wine, lemon juice and chicken bouillon. Add herbs, spices and salt. Cover and simmer for 45 minutes.

Spaghetti à la Don Juan

There must be some reason for the popularity of spaghetti – have you ever thought what it might be? In eighteenth-century France, Parmesan cheese was thought to be especially sexually stimulating, which might be part of the reason.

- 1 lb spaghetti
- 2 tablespoons olive oil
- 1 small onion, peeled and chopped
- 1 clove garlic, crushed
- 2 sprigs thyme, or ½ teaspoon dried thyme
- 1 lb carrots, scraped and chopped
- 1 lb tomatoes, chopped
- 1 cup water
- Parmesan cheese

Bring some water to the boil in a saucepan. Add spaghetti, lower heat and cook until tender. Drain and keep aside. Heat oil in a pan, add onion, garlic and thyme. Stir for a few seconds, then add carrots and tomatoes. Pour in the cup of water. When the carrots are cooked, place in a blender and purée. Pour this sauce on to the spaghetti, sprinkle with parsley and parmesan cheese and serve.

Hidden charms

Here is your opportunity to reveal them at last. . . .

- 1 green papaya, unpeeled, cut in half lengthwise
- 1 clove garlic, crushed
- 1 small onion, peeled and chopped
- 1 tablespoon olive oil
- ½ lb lean minced beef
- 1 green pepper, seeded and chopped
- ¼ lb mushrooms, thinly sliced
- salt and ground black pepper to taste
- a little rosemary
- pinch cinnamon

Remove and discard seeds in the papaya. Put the papaya in boiling water and boil for 10 minutes. Remove and place on baking tray. Stir-fry the garlic and onion in olive oil. Add minced beef and fry for about 15 minutes until the meat is browned. Add green peppers, mushrooms, salt and pepper. Sprinkle with rosemary and cinnamon. Fill the papaya halves with the meat mixture. Put in a warm oven and bake for 30 minutes at 180°C (350°F, gas mark 4).

Cupid's casserole

There are enough potent ingredients in this dish to safely ensure a direct hit. . . .

- ½ lb calf's liver, chopped into pieces
- 2 cooking apples, unpeeled, chopped
- 1 Spanish onion, peeled and sliced
- 2 tomatoes, sliced
- 2 bacon slices, chopped into small pieces
- 1 oz white wine
- 1 teaspoon paprika
- salt and ground black pepper to taste

Place the liver pieces on a bed of cooking apples in a casserole dish. Put the onions and tomatoes on top; sprinkle with bacon. Pour the wine over and season with paprika, salt and pepper. Cook in oven 180°C (350°C, gas mark 4) for 20–30 minutes.

Tipsy steak

It's all right for the steak to be tipsy, but not for you. It is impossible to be seductive while concentrating on staying upright.

- 1 lb braising steak, cut into small cubes
- 2 tablespoons olive oil
- 6–8 small onions, peeled but left whole
- ½ bottle red wine
- salt and ground black pepper to taste
- 2 tablespoons chopped spring onions

Sauté the steak in olive oil, add onions and pour in the wine. Cover and simmer for about 45 minutes. Season with salt and pepper. Cook for a further 10 minutes and sprinkle with spring onions.

Ginger beef

The exotic East has cast more than one spell over the western imagination. Food, of course, is one. And sex is another. . . .

- 1 lb braising steak, sliced into 1 inch strips
- 4 tablespoons soya sauce
- 2 tablespoons olive oil
- 6 small onions, peeled and sliced
- 1 oz ginger root, thinly sliced
- 2 tomatoes, chopped
- 2 tablespoons chopped spring onions

Marinate the meat in the soya sauce for 30 minutes. Heat the oil in a pan, add onions and ginger, and stir-fry until the onions are soft but not browned. Add the meat and tomatoes. Cook on a low heat for 30–45 minutes. Sprinkle with spring onions and serve with rice.

Stroganoff Karenina

Treat him like a count to this exotic and exciting dish – preferably served whilst lying in front of a log fire on a bearskin rug as the first snows fall outside the window – and watch those flames grow higher!

- ½ lb rump steak, cut into small pieces
- salt and ground black pepper, to taste
- 1 oz butter
- 1 shallot, chopped
- ½ lb mushrooms, sliced
- 2 tablespoons tomato purée
- 2 tablespoons natural yoghurt
- 2 glasses beef stock
- pinch nutmeg

Sprinkle the steak with salt and black pepper. Melt the butter in a pan and sauté the meat. Add shallot and mushrooms. Cook for 5–8 minutes, then stir in the tomato purée and yoghurt. Add the beef stock, sprinkle with nutmeg and simmer for about 45 minutes.

Steak au poivre

You should use as much fresh ground pepper as you can bear; it will arouse passion to unlimited heights.

- 2 teaspoons freshly ground black pepper
- 12 oz rump steak, cut into 2 pieces
- salt to taste
- 2 tablespoons olive oil
- 2 large onions, peeled and cut into rings
- 2 tablespoons chopped spring onions

With the back of a spoon press the black pepper into the steak and sprinkle with salt. Pour the oil into a large frying pan. Cover the bottom of the pan with onions and put the steak on top. Cook on a low heat for about 1 hour, turning 2 or 3 times. Sprinkle with spring onions and serve with a green salad.

Steak tartare

The eating of raw steak was popular with the Tartars who would put meat under their horses' saddles, so that after a good day's rape and pillage, the steaks would be well pounded and ready to eat. This would rapidly replenish their physical and sexual energy.

- 2 anchovy fillets, chopped into small pieces
- 1 teaspoon vinegar
- 1 teaspoon olive oil
- 1 egg yolk
- 1 lb sirloin steak, coarsely ground
- 1 teaspoon Dijon mustard
- 2 small onions, chopped finely
- 2 teaspoons capers
- salt and black pepper to taste
- 2 tablespoons chopped fresh parsley

Mix the anchovy fillets, vinegar, oil and egg yolk together. Add the steak, mustard, onions and capers. Season with salt and pepper. Mix well with a fork and sprinkle with parsley. Chill for at least 2 hours before serving.

11. Sinful sweets

The finale to a meal – if to nothing else – should be light and delicate. These puddings should be served away from the dinner table, preferably on a divan, which is more relaxing, intimate, and likely to lead to more than clearing up. They are easy and quick to prepare, though a few, such as sorbets and water-ices, should be prepared a day or so in advance. They are all deliciously appetizing and will seduce any virgin or not-so-virgin palate. I have not included any cakes as these are inclined to be heavy and hinder your activities. No coffee, either, as this will bring your partner swiftly back to reality and ruin the erotic atmosphere you have so carefully created.

These desserts are only for that special occasion and so are not really fattening as they are not part of your everyday diet. They are also light and easily digested. They should be served with a sweet white wine.

Succulent sorbet

Apples are not the only fruits to lead you into temptation....

6 oz strawberries
4 oz sugar
4 tablespoons water
juice of ½ lemon
1 egg white, whisked till frothy

Place the strawberries, sugar and water in a saucepan and simmer until puréed. Leave to cool. Stir in the lemon juice and pour into an ice-cube tray. Half-freeze then empty into a bowl. Add the egg-white, mix thoroughly and refreeze.

Mango and gin sorbet

4 large ripe mangoes, peeled and stoned
1 small glass water
4 oz brown sugar
1 tablespoon gin
1 egg white, whisked until frothy

Put the mangoes into a saucepan, add water and sugar and cook until they form a pulp. Add the gin and purée the fruit in a blender. Freeze for 2 hours. Then put the purée into a bowl and beat well with a fork. Fold in the egg white and refreeze.

Eve's ice

Apples, which feature largely in just about everyone's legends as a symbol of sex, sexuality or rejuvenation, are the secret ingredients of this unusual dessert.

1 lb apples, sliced (but not peeled or seeded)
juice of 1 lemon
2 tablespoons honey
1 small glass apple juice
1 stick cinnamon

Cook the apples with lemon juice, honey, apple juice and cinnamon stick until they are soft. Remove the cinnamon stick and purée the fruit and its syrup in a blender. Freeze for about 2 hours. Remove the purée from the freezer, beat with a fork and return to freezer. (It is important to include the peel and seeds of the apples for the charm to work.)

What-the-hell parfait

Sinfully rich, this is just the dessert when you really feel like letting go.

8 oz raspberries
4 scoops vanilla ice-cream
2 tablespoons whipped cream
2 tablespoons grated coconut

Mix together for marinade:
2 tablespoons brown sugar
1 small glass kirsch

Marinate the raspberries overnight. Place 1 scoop of ice-cream in each dish. Drain the raspberries and add to the ice-cream. Cover with another scoop of ice-cream, add 1 tablespoon whipped cream; sprinkle with coconut and serve immediately.

Banana split

Obviously, this is not the dessert for every night of the week, but if you're really into something both different and nostalgic. . . .

2 bananas, halved
vanilla ice-cream
4 tablespoons whipped cream
2 wafers

Place 2 banana halves in each dish; fill the space between the banana halves with 2 scoops of ice-cream. Decorate with whipped cream and wafers.

Caribbean sundae

The next best thing to lying on a white sandy beach beneath a palm tree, the water lapping at your feet and the guitars playing something romantic.

4 passion fruits
8 oz chopped pineapple, fresh
   or tinned
1 banana
lemon juice
vanilla ice-cream
2 tablespoons grated coconut

Cut the passion fruit in half and spoon contents into a bowl; add the pineapple. Slice the banana and sprinkle with lemon juice before adding to the other fruit. Put the fruit mixture into 2 dishes, cover each with 1 scoop of vanilla ice-cream, sprinkle with coconut and serve.

Lovers' dream salads

Take your pick. . . .

No. 1

2 peaches, peeled, stoned and sliced
6 oz pineapple cubes
1 pear, sliced and cored
2 kiwi fruit, sliced
2 tablespoons sunflower seeds
1 teaspoon cinnamon
juice of 1 lemon
1 tablespoon honey

Place all ingredients in a bowl. Toss and serve with natural yoghurt.

No. 2

1 pear, peeled and sliced
1 small bunch black grapes
1 orange, segmented
4 prunes, stoned, cut into 4–6 pieces
1 small glass peach nectar
juice of 1 lemon
1 tablespoon kirsch

Put the fruit, peach nectar and lemon juice into a bowl. Mix well. Sprinkle with kirsch and serve chilled.

No. 3

2 cups tinned jackfruit pulp or fresh papaya
1 banana, thinly sliced
crushed ice
double cream
1 tablespoon grated coconut

Put the fruit in tall, chilled glasses. Add crushed ice, top with double cream, sprinkle with coconut and serve.

No. 4

1 cup lychees, stoned
2 guavas, sliced
2 persimmons, sliced
Grand Marnier

Mix the fruit together, lace with Grand Marnier and serve.

No. 5

2 cups wild strawberries
2 tablespoons double cream
Cherry liqueur

Divide the strawberries into 2 bowls. Cover each with a tablespoon of double cream and a few drops of cherry liqueur.

Passionate dreams

The nicest sort of dreams to have in anyone's recipe book. . . .

2 passion fruits
1 dessertspoon brown sugar
1 tablespoon brown rum
2 peaches, stoned and sliced
1 pear, sliced
1 banana, sliced
whipped cream

Cut the passion fruit in halves and spoon contents into an ovenproof dish. Add brown sugar, rum, and the other fruit. Place in a warm oven. When you are ready for dessert, serve with huge dollops of cream.

Spiced grapefruit

Grapefruit can do more than just wake you up at breakfast – with the right blend of spices they are the perfect end to a romantic meal for two.

1 grapefruit
1 tablespoon brown sugar
pinch cinnamon
pinch ground nutmeg
2 dessertspoons Crème de Cacao
a little butter
2 maraschino cherries

Cut the grapefruit in half and segment carefully with a knife, removing core from centre. Sprinkle with sugar and spices. Pour 1 dessertspoon of liqueur over each half; put a knob of butter on each and place in a warm oven when you serve the main course. Just before you serve the dessert decorate with cherries.

Not too heavy, not too sweet, and definitely not too ordinary, these are the perfect desserts to end a meal that is only a beginning. . . .

Sweet sensation

2 cooking apples	butter
raisins	1 small glass white wine
4 cloves	1 teaspoon Calvados
brown sugar to taste	

Remove and discard the core from the middle of the apples. Place them in an ovenproof dish and fill each with raisins and 2 cloves. Sprinkle with sugar and place a knob of butter on each. Pour the wine and Calvados into the dish and bake in oven 180°C (350°F, gas mark 4) for about 25 minutes. Serve hot.

A taste of honey

2 bananas	4 teaspoons honey
2 tablespoons lemon juice	butter
2 teaspoons brown sugar	2 teaspoons rum

Peel the bananas and cut in half lengthwise. Sprinkle with lemon juice, then roll in sugar. Pour a teaspoon of honey on each of the halves and place the other banana half on top. Put each banana on a piece of tin foil, pour a teaspoon of rum over and top with a knob of butter. Close the foil parcels and bake in oven 190°C (375°F, gas mark 5) for 15 minutes.

Eastern delight

Scheherazade kept up her Sultan's interest with storytelling – but you can go straight to his heart with this delicious offering.

½ lb sago
2 tablespoons moong beans, soaked overnight
4 whole cardamoms
2 tablespoons raisins
1 tablespoon grated coconut
1 small glass milk
2 tablespoons brown sugar

Wash the sago, cover with water, add moong beans and cardamom and cook over a moderate heat, stirring all the time. When the sago is half cooked, add raisins, coconut milk and sugar. Cooking time is about 30–45 minutes in all.

Crème renversée à la indienne

'Love is a burning flame', they say – now's your chance to set the night alight!

1 pint skimmed milk
10 cardamoms
4 eggs
2 tablespoons brown sugar
1 tablespoon dark rum

For sugar syrup:
juice of 1 lemon
4 tablespoons brown sugar
2 tablespoons water

Boil milk with the cardamoms and put aside. Beat the eggs and the 2 tablespoons sugar together, add the warm milk and mix well.

Make the sugar syrup by mixing the lemon juice, sugar and water together over a low heat until the sugar dissolves. Bring to the boil, then pour the syrup into an ovenproof dish. Add the milk and egg mixture. Cook in a *bain marie* in a moderate oven for about 45 minutes. Allow to cool. Turn into a bowl and chill in the fridge. Before serving, pour the rum over and flambé.

12. Before and after drinks

How many times a day does someone say, 'Have a little drink, it'll make you feel better', or, 'What you need is a cup of tea'? How many times have you said it yourself – this week alone? Whether you are feeling down or feeling ill, feeling tired or feeling edgy, having a drink is the simple solution. Second only to mum's home-made soup as the perfect cure for everything from heartache to headache, having a drink – whether gin or ginger ale – is the perfect way to relax and perk up at the same time.

The drinks in this section are intended to stimulate your sexual drive and to help you to relax. The aphrodisiac tisanes – though traditionally used by men for their health-giving properties – are as good for the goose as for the gander and are now making a popular come-back as their healing and calming properties are rediscovered. Though they may not make you want to dance all night to old love songs or rip your clothes off and run around the room doing your Isadore Duncan impersonation (as a bottle of neat Tequila might encourage you to do), they will go far to stirring up the glowing embers in your heart and, alternatively, won't make you wish you were someone else the next day.

On the other hand, of course, there are situations for which the perfect drink can be nothing but an elegant cocktail or a sophisticated wine. A little alcohol goes a long way towards releasing tensions and inhibitions and helping you to throw caution to the winds. But a lot of alcohol will only put you to sleep or put you out of commission, so go easy. Drunken people simply do not make good drivers, good cooks, or good lovers. It's just the way things are.

A good wine, however, always helps to warm things up and starts balls rolling. It was a necessary feature at all Roman orgies, and though there is no sense in getting as carried away as that, a glass or two will do a lot more good than harm. For very special occasions, of course, there is only champagne. But only you can decide which occasions those are. . . .

Aphrodisiac tisanes

Blast of passion

2 oz yellow ginseng root, sliced
1 oz ginger root, sliced
1 pint water

Simmer the ginseng and ginger root in water for about 45 minutes. Sweeten with honey if required.

Elixir of life

1 tablespoon sesame seeds
1 tablespoon sunflower seeds
1 oz alfalfa
½ pint spring water
2 oz ginseng wine
2 teaspoons honey

Combine the sesame seeds, sunflower seeds and alfalfa together in a blender. Place the mixture with the spring water in a saucepan and bring gently to the boil. Cover and simmer for 30 minutes. Add ginseng wine and honey.

Charm nectar

5 dates, finely chopped
5 figs, finely chopped
1 oz liquorice root
½ pint water
2 tablespoons honey
½ melon, peeled, seeded and cut into chunks
pinch ground cinnamon

Place the dates, figs, liquorice root and spring water in a saucepan. Simmer for 15 minutes. Add honey, melon and cinnamon and whizz in blender.

Love philtre

1 small bunch citronella leaves (also known as lemon balm) including the roots
1 oz root ginger
1 tablespoon brown sugar
1 pint water

Place the citronella with the ginger, sugar and water in a saucepan and bring slowly to the boil. Cover and simmer for 15 minutes. Drink last thing at night.

Lift-up

For rooting out any lonely feelings.

1 handful dandelion roots, roasted
¾ pint water
1½ teaspoons honey

Place the dandelion roots and water in a saucepan, bring slowly to the boil and simmer for about 10 minutes. Add honey, strain and serve hot.

Decoction delight

The manglier is a tree that grows near the sea in tropical islands, the bark of which is a legendary aphrodisiac. Next time you go off on that exotic holiday, make it an erotic one as well.

1 small piece bark or branch of manglier
¾ pint water

Bring the water to the boil, add the manglier and simmer for about 15 minutes. Drink 2 cups first thing each morning. (The natives swear by it.)

Some like it hot

Others like it plain sizzling. . . .

Hot rum

½ pint water
1 glass old rum (the size of the
   glass is up to you)
½ stick cinnamon
juice of ½ lemon
1 tablespoon brown sugar

Bring the water to the boil, stir in the rum, cinnamon, lemon juice and sugar. Serve immediately.

Spicy fruit punch

1 pint orange juice
½ pint pineapple juice
½ pint apple juice
¼ pint water
a few thin slices ginger root
¼ teaspoon mace

pinch nutmeg
¼ teaspoon ground cinnamon
1 orange, sliced
1 apple, sliced
1 cup cubed pineapple

Place the fruit juices, water, ginger and spices into a saucepan. Bring slowly to the boil, then simmer gently for about 5 minutes. Serve in warm glasses with slices of orange, apple and pineapple.

Mulled wine

1 bottle light red wine
peel and juice of 1 orange
1 teaspoon ground coriander

4 whole cloves
½ cinnamon stick
2 tablespoons brandy

Place the wine, orange juice, peel and spices in a saucepan. Simmer gently for about 10 minutes. Add brandy. Strain the liquid and serve in warm glasses.

High spirits

These recipes give only proportions. I am leaving actual amounts to individual discretion.

Orange blossom

½ dry gin
½ orange juice

Shake and strain into a cocktail glass.

Tingling sensation

Fill a couple of tall glasses with champagne. Add a nip of brandy, dash of angostura and a slice of orange.

Between the sheets

⅓ brandy
⅓ white rum
⅓ Cointreau
dash lemon juice

Shake and strain into a cocktail glass.

Forbidden love

⅓ forbidden fruit (apple) liqueur
⅓ Grand Marnier
⅓ old rum

Shake and strain into a cocktail glass.

Bunny hug

⅓ whisky
⅓ gin
⅓ Pernod

Shake and strain into a cocktail glass.

Swinging Ginny

⅔ gin
⅓ lemon juice
sparkling mineral water

Pour gin and lemon juice into a tall glass, add sparkling mineral water, crushed ice and a twist of lemon rind.

Refreshments

For those languorous summer evenings that go on into the night. . . .

Sparkling peach nectar

2 large ripe peaches
2 tablespoons Grand Marnier
1 bottle champagne, chilled

Slice the peaches roughly into a blender, pour in the Grand Marnier, blend until smooth. Pour 2 tablespoons of the nectar into each champagne glass, top up with champagne.

Papaya sensation

1 small ripe papaya, peeled and seeded
1 bottle sparkling white wine, chilled

Spoon the papaya pulp into a blender and whizz until runny and smooth. Half-fill a couple of tall glasses (keeping the rest for top-ups) and fill up with sparkling wine.

Shocking pink

2 vanilla pods
1 pint milk
1 tablespoon gelatine
2 tablespoons sugar
1 teaspoon pink colouring
1 small glass water
crushed ice

Add the vanilla pods to the milk and bring gently to the boil. Remove the pods and allow to cool. Chill. Meanwhile put the gelatine, sugar and colouring with the water into a saucepan. Stir over a low heat until both the gelatine and sugar dissolve. Mix with the milk and chill. Give it a good stir before serving in tall glasses with crushed ice.

Cool virgin sip

½ cucumber, peeled and chopped
½ pint natural yoghurt
salt and white pepper to taste
a few sprigs mint

Blend cucumber, natural yoghurt, salt and pepper. Serve in tall glasses with straws, garnish with fresh sprigs of mint.

13. Exercises

An exercise by any other name is still the only way to get your body into the shape it would like to be in. The exercises in this section are not just to make you supple, strong, flexible and fit, but to add even more enjoyment to your sex life. The yoga positions, the basic exercises, and the exotic dances described here, when practised correctly and regularly, should especially tone up those parts of you that get their biggest work-out during love-making, as well as helping to stimulate and rejuvenate sexual glands and organs. Once you've kicked off both your shoes and your inhibitions, they will not only help you to relax and to ease the tensions and anxieties with which we all contend, but will, slowly but surely, make you more aware of your body in all its sensuous glory.

The best results will be obtained by doing these exercises for at least 30 minutes every day for the first 4 weeks. After that, 3 to 4 sessions a week should be enough to keep you in shape, your senses tingling and your cells all bubbling. Exercise in a well-aired room, and remember to breathe deeply as you do your movements. This helps the circulation, reduces emotional tension and soothes frazzled nerves. Inhale as you come into the exercise, and exhale as you come out. In between exercises, lie down on the floor and relax. Do not rush through the exercises or over-exert yourself, just take your time, enjoy yourself, and revel in your own sensuality.

By toning up your body you will not only increase your poise, magnetism and joy in living, but you will become fully aware of your body and its sexual energies – and will find yourself enjoying sex more. Since it is the best all-round exercise, a greater enjoyment of sex will increase your overall vitality – which, of course, will increase your overall enjoyment. This is a non-vicious cycle. Sexual activity is ideal for developing stamina, suppleness and muscular strength – even more so than swimming – and is also effective in shaping and tightening the body as it exercises all the major muscles of the abdomen and limbs. It is also the best aerobic exercise around; one 20–30 minute session being as good as a 1-mile walk, and probably a lot more fun. The rhythmic and vigorous effort used in love-making also demands a greater supply of oxygen in the blood and therefore exercises both the heart and the lungs as well. Personally, I would much rather spend 30 minutes in a candle-lit bedroom with the object of my affections than 30 minutes jogging through the park in the snow.

And remember. No matter how far away from your hands your toes may seem when you begin exercising, once you get in shape it is all that much easier to enjoy the shape you're in.

Basic keep fit

Breathing exercises

The first two breathing exercises here should be done at the start of your session. They make you more aware of both your breathing and your body during the exercises and they help develop your diaphragm and fill your muscles and brain with plenty of oxygen. Oxygen is a great source of energy. It influences emotions, helps with food digestion and rids the body of waste matter. (Make the most of it and pep up your body and your mind!)

Spatial breathing
This is to help you become aware of your 'space' – the area you influence and in which you radiate feelings and thoughts that can deeply affect your partner.

Lie down on your back, close your eyes and visualize air entering and leaving the body. Feel your back move as you inhale and exhale. (If you can't feel your back moving, you are still out of tune with your body.) Spread out your arms and imagine that you are expanding and discovering the space you influence.

Abdominal breathing
This helps develop the ability to use your stomach muscles, especially in the belly dancercise later in this chapter.

Stand with your back straight and your arms loosely relaxed at your sides. Expel all the breath in your body by contracting the abdomen as you exhale through the nose letting the head and shoulders relax forward a little. Now start to inhale gently, allowing the abdomen to expand first, then the diaphragm and finally the chest. Hold your breath for a few seconds and then exhale slowly, reversing the process: the chest will sink down and contract, followed by the diaphragm and the abdomen, then let the head and shoulders relax once more. Repeat the movement as many times as you wish.

Rhythmic breathing
This is a tonic to the mind which brings you in tune with the universe and makes you forget your loneliness. Try it while jogging, bicycling or just walking.

Breathe to the rhythm of in 1, 2, 3 and out 1, 2, 3 and later increase the count to 4 then 5 and so on.

The bust sequence

This will keep the breasts firm and shapely; or tone up sagging breasts. You will never have to feel self-conscious when trying on a bathing suit again.

* Stand, feet wide apart, arms hanging loosely by your sides, then raise both arms forward, upwards, backwards and sideways, in a circular motion, brushing your ears with your arms as you go past. Repeat 15 times.

* Roll first one shoulder then the other, 10 times each. Relax for a while; then roll both shoulders together backwards then forward.

* Raise your left arm behind your head and with your right hand pull it towards your right hand side. Then change hands and repeat towards the other side. Repeat 10 times each side.

* Lie face downwards and rest your chin on the floor. Put your fingertips beneath your shoulders, hands pointing inwards, elbows bent. Holding tummy muscles in, press hands on floor and slowly straighten arms so that your thighs, torso and head leave the floor in just one movement. Still keeping your body straight, lower yourself towards the floor. Repeat 8 times.

* Lie down on the floor and relax for a few seconds before moving on to the next exercise.

The knee kiss

This is for suppleness and to strengthen the abdominal muscles. Sexual vigour is largely dependent on the healthy condition of the abdomen.

* Lie on your back on the floor with both legs extended. Inhale as you bend one knee and draw it towards your chest, at the same time raise your upper back, head and neck off the floor. Now reach for your knee with your hands and draw it towards your face. From here you should be able to kiss your knee easily!

    Exhale as you release this position slowly until you are lying flat on your back again. Rest for a few seconds. Then try the movement with the other leg.

* Stand up, feet together, raise the left knee with your hands and bring it towards your face. Repeat with the right knee. Repeat 10 times with each knee.

Curl up

* Lie flat on your back, knees bent, feet together flat on the ground. Slowly raise head and shoulders by curling them up, keeping the rest of you flat. Hold to a count of 8, then slowly uncurl down again. Repeat 4 times.

The Frog

This helps to stretch the inner thigh.

* Lie flat on your back; bend your knees outwards, press the soles of your feet together and lower your thighs to the floor.
  Relax the inner thighs and press the small of your back into the floor. Hold the position for as long as is comfortable. Repeat 5 times.

Abdominal exercises

These are worthwhile as they flatten and tone up your tummy muscles. The exercises are progressive – they move from one stage to the next gradually so as not to strain the abdominal muscles.

* Sit on the front part of a chair, legs straight, heels on the floor, lean back and grip the sides of the seat for support. Bend the knees and bring the front of the thighs up to squeeze gently against the body. Repeat 8 times.

* Do the same exercise with the legs held straight.

* Lie on your back, knees slightly bent, with your feet tucked under a heavy chair or sofa, arms stretched backwards. Reach forward very slowly with your arms to bring yourself into a sitting position. Bring your hands down on to your legs and lower your chin to your chest. Then roll back slowly letting the back touch the floor first and then the head. Relax, then repeat 8 times.

* Lie flat on your back, with the legs and feet together, arms by your sides. Repeat the movement in the third stage but this

time do not tuck your feet under a settee, but try to do the movement unaided.

The pelvic tilt sequence

Any tension in the pelvis affects your sex life. The following pelvic exercises eliminate stress in that area, including lower back problems, they strengthen your pelvic muscles and are excellent for a woman's sexual comfort.

* Lie flat on your back on the floor with arms relaxed at your sides. Bend your knees and keep your feet flat on the floor. Flatten your entire spine against the floor and raise your buttocks off the floor by contracting the muscles of your abdomen and buttocks. Hold as long as is comfortable then roll the pelvis back again. Inhale as you lift your pelvis; exhale as you let it come down again. Repeat 10 times.

* Lie flat on your back, knees bent a hip width apart, feet flat on the floor. Raise your buttocks up off the floor, contracting the muscles of your abdomen and buttocks. Then close your legs very slowly until your knees touch each other. Hold for a count of 5; open your legs slowly as you let your pelvis roll back again. Repeat 10 times.

* Still lying flat on your back with knees bent, raise your buttocks up off the floor. Contract the muscles of your abdomen and buttocks and tilt the pelvis to the left; relax then contract and tilt to the right. Repeat 10 times.

The pelvic tenser
* Lie flat on your stomach with your chin on the ground and arms at your sides. Tighten buttock muscles and stomach muscles simultaneously and hold for a slow count of 5. Relax, then repeat as often as is comfortable.

Vaginal contractions

These also help tighten the pelvic floor.

* Lie on your back on the floor, contract the vagina, hold for a count of 4, relax and repeat 15 times.

The bum roll

This is for firming up buttocks.

* Lie on your back, keeping your spine flat on the floor with arms extended wide at shoulder level. Bend your knees and keep your feet together flat on the floor. Slowly swing your knees over from side to side, keeping the upper half of your body flat on the ground. Repeat 15 times.

* Lie on your back as above. Bend your knees and bring them up towards your chest. Then roll your hips from side to side. Repeat 15 times.

Beginner's yoga

Yoga is a very good way to relax and revitalize the mind and body and also benefits the internal organs and glandular system. Practise regularly and you will soon notice a general improvement in your health and most particularly in your sex life. In oriental philosophy, sexual union is considered the highest form of yoga – hence the name yoga, which means 'to make union'.

Early morning or in the evening are the best times for yoga. You should practise in a quiet room so that you can concentrate fully. Each movement should be done slowly and gently so that you are in complete control. The postures are supposed to stretch and relax the body, not to exhaust it. Some positions may prove difficult at first but go only as far as you feel comfortable. You will pull or strain your muscles and ligaments if you try to do too much too quickly but, as your muscles become loosened and more flexible, you will find that it is easier for your body to adopt these positions.

Breathing is also an important part of yoga and should be practised at the same time as the movements. It will help to remove mental stress and tension, relaxing you completely. You will become more aware of your breathing and the energies inside you, which will help your concentration. Breathe slowly and deeply and try to adapt your rhythm of breathing to that of the exercise.

Yoga should be practised as a creative activity to help you develop a deep awareness of your body. Try visualizing the flow of energy through the position while you are practising and this will help channel energy through your whole body. Yoga will therefore help to improve your mental as well as your physical condition.

Cupid's Bow

This is good for the abdominal and back muscles, making the back supple, strong and beautiful. It tightens buttocks, thighs and backs of arms; strengthens shoulders, arms and neck, and firms and develops the chest. It is very effective in strengthening the gonads, which govern sexuality.

* Lie on your stomach, reach back to hold your ankles with your hands, bend the knees but keep the elbows straight. Raise chest and legs off the ground and rock backwards and forwards 10 times. Relax with your arms by your sides and elbows slightly bent to relax the shoulders. Repeat 10 times breathing normally throughout.

The Locust

This is excellent for treating sexual debility and it is beneficial for the bladder and sex glands but you should not attempt it if you suffer from any heart condition.

* Lie flat on your stomach and relax for a few seconds. Then bring the legs and feet together and rest your face on the point of your chin. Straighten the elbows and make fists with your hands, thumbs towards the floor. Push down hard with the fists and raise the legs, keeping the knees straight and the feet together. Hold your position for a count of 5, then slowly lower your legs to the floor. Relax completely before repeating this exercise 5 times.

The Headstand
This will rejuvenate the sexual glands and organs. It also provides an all-over toning, improves the blood circulation and does wonders for hair, scalp and skin.

* At first practise kneeling with your weight firmly resting on forearms and elbows, hands on the floor, fingers interlocked cupping your head to keep it steady. Rise on your toes and, with bent knees, move slowly forward until you feel the weight of your body balanced on your arms. After a few weeks practising this position, when you feel comfortable and can control your balance, raise your legs slowly while your hands hold your head steady. Practise near a wall for support, if necessary.

The Fish
This helps release tension in the upper back, strengthens the neck and the whole spine and stretches the muscles of the thighs. It also improves sexual energy.

* Sit on your heels, knees together, and lean your torso back, keeping your knees on the floor. Rest the weight of your torso on to your elbows. Next lower your head towards the floor, relaxing the head and neck backwards. Gradually slide your elbows towards your feet so that your torso arches towards the ceiling. Slowly let the top of your head sink to the floor so that eventually you raise your arms off the floor and let your head and the arch in your back support your torso. Inhale and raise both arms in a large arc up towards the ceiling, then back over your head. Take a deep breath, opening up chest and back as you arch. Exhale as you bring your arms back down to your sides. Repeat 4 times.

The Plough
This is excellent for those trying to slim as it stimulates the thyroid gland for weight control. It also aids the balance of hormonal levels in the body, tones up the organs and improves health and beauty.

* Lie on your back, arms at your sides, legs and feet together. Turn the palms of your hands towards the floor and raise

your legs, keeping the knees straight. Bring the legs over as far as they will go comfortably. Hold the position for as long as you feel comfortable. Come out of the plough by bending the knees in towards the chest and tucking the feet in. Hold your waist with your hands and slowly roll out. Bring the legs smoothly back down to the floor. Relax for a few seconds. Repeat 5 times.

Body language

Getting into shape does not always mean exercising. If you are easily bored by exercises, there are erotic ways which are fun to tone up abdominal and pelvic muscles. Why not try African and/or belly dancing! You will achieve a well-articulated pelvis, increased sexual agility and, at the same time, become more sensuous as you are more aware of your body and inner body sensations.

In belly or African dances there are no rigid rules. Once you have learned fully to relax your body as you move and your inhibitions have disappeared, you can create your own movements – imagine you have a beautiful body and the rest will be easy.

Belly dancing is a dance of the flesh, so use mirrors and play evocative music to help you move more sinuously. Your movements should be flowing. Let yourself go and release your muscles; you cannot belly dance if you are tense. Try to move your arms like snakes and keep them close to your body. Use your hands to accentuate the movements of your hips, pelvis or belly. These areas play a particularly important part in love-making. Great demands are made upon them and loss of muscle tone in the abdomen and thighs, and a blocked-up pelvis – usually the cause of lower back tension and pain – will not improve your love-making. Twenty minutes belly dancing every day tones up the muscles and relaxes the mind. You will become more graceful every day and the end result will be a more beautiful and sensuous you.

African dancing is for the more energetic. It is a form of manifesting energy and at the same time it helps you move erotically. It is the body's rhythmic response to music. Your spine and pelvis move beautifully. You move your body sensually and openly express your sexuality as in the 'Séga' which is danced by the inhabitants of the tropical islands (Mauritius) off the south-east coast of Africa. The experience is unique.

14. Oriental massage – a sensual, luxurious treat

Massage is a delicious way of communicating with your partner, and adds a deep intimacy to your relationship. Just the act of touching provides the inner nourishment the body needs and promotes well-being and relaxation. In the East, it forms part of the art of love and is an important part of the life of both Japanese geishas and maharajas' courtesans. Suggesting that you rub someone's back for him is always a good way of letting him know the way your thoughts are moving.

The art of massage has been known for thousands of years. It is instinctive to the hands to soothe and unravel stress with a series of fluid, enveloping movements; this massage is particularly invigorating and therapeutic, and should be reciprocal. It can eliminate many sexual problems, such as lack of sexual interest and impotency, when practised regularly and it is an excellent way to tune in to your lover's body. It can be an effective part of foreplay to relax and arouse the body and certain areas – such as the toes, the area around the heel and the ears – are particularly good massage points. They are linked to the sexual zones and are erotically stimulating.

When you are massaging your partner, try to feel confident and you will find that the movements will come intuitively to your hands. Your partner should surrender himself to you completely and you should participate with your whole body by synchronizing your movement with your breathing, thus adding rhythm to your action.

It is quite possible for you to massage yourself. This is especially good after a bath or shower when your body is warm and relaxed and hips and thighs will particularly benefit, as they are the areas where fatty tissues and cellulite tend to collect. Use circular movements if you use a massage glove, but be careful not to bruise yourself. You can also use your fingers to pick up muscle and knead for a few minutes, until your skin blushes slightly. This way will tone up lax muscles and keep your skin supple.

Herbal pleasure

Massage influences oil absorption, so use one of the aphrodisiac oils listed below with a base massage oil. These essential oils have a particularly strong effect on the central nervous system as they affect mood, thought and emotion. Combined with massage and shiatsu† they possess a unique power to seduce the mind and balance your inner rhythms.

Basil and lavender – to balance nervous emotional conditions.
Black pepper – for warmth and strength.
Clary sage – has a sweet, nutty, long-lasting perfume; it can also be used in the bath to revitalize you after a long and exhausting day.
Ginseng – for increased sexual drive.
Mustard – for warmth during cold winter nights.
Patchouli and Rose – to seduce.
Rosemary – a very good stimulant where there is apathy, debility and physical fatigue.
Sweet orange – is especially refreshing and uplifting.
Ylang ylang – for frigidity and impotency.

† *Shiatsu* is a Japanese massage based on the same energy system as acupuncture. Instead of needles, thumbs and fingers are used on the pressure points which influence the harmonious flow of energy through the body via the meridian lines.

Other oils:
Huile de coprah – to treat impotency; massage the abdomen, using downward movements, for 15 minutes daily over a 10-day period.

The back

The back is erotic and can be deeply sensual without being overtly sexual. Back massage is very soothing and relaxes the whole body as the system of nerves which radiates from the spinal cord reaches almost every part of you.

The back stroke
* Stand at one end of the couch behind your partner's head. Place your hands on each side of the spine and, starting from the top – fingers slightly curved so you can dig in – press with your palms and glide your hands down the back. Then bring them smoothly back to the starting point. Repeat 5 times. The last time, bunch your hands into fists and use your knuckles to glide down the back; lean into your partner's back muscles with your full body weight, opening your hands when you reach the lower back.

The lower back
* Stand beside your partner's hips. Start from the sacrum and, using the palms of your hands, stretch the muscles on each side of the lower back outwards following the pelvic bone. Repeat 4 times.

Back wring
This is a lovely way to finish your work on the back. Make a wringing or twisting movement across your partner's back with your hands. Start from the lower back and move upwards and downwards a couple of times.

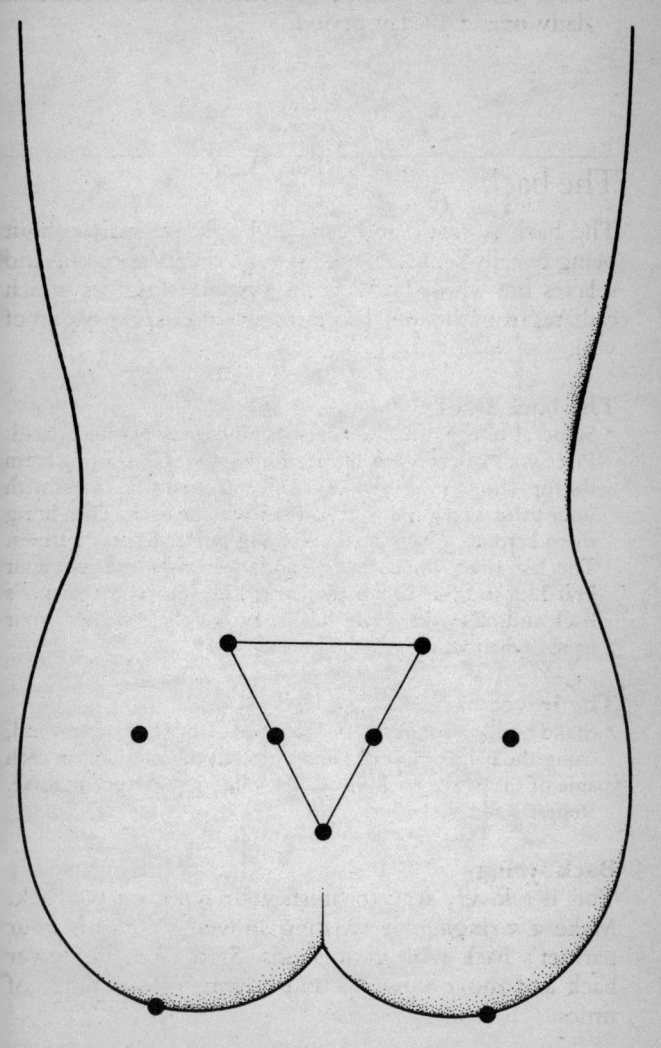

The triangle of Venus

Pressure points for the sexual organs

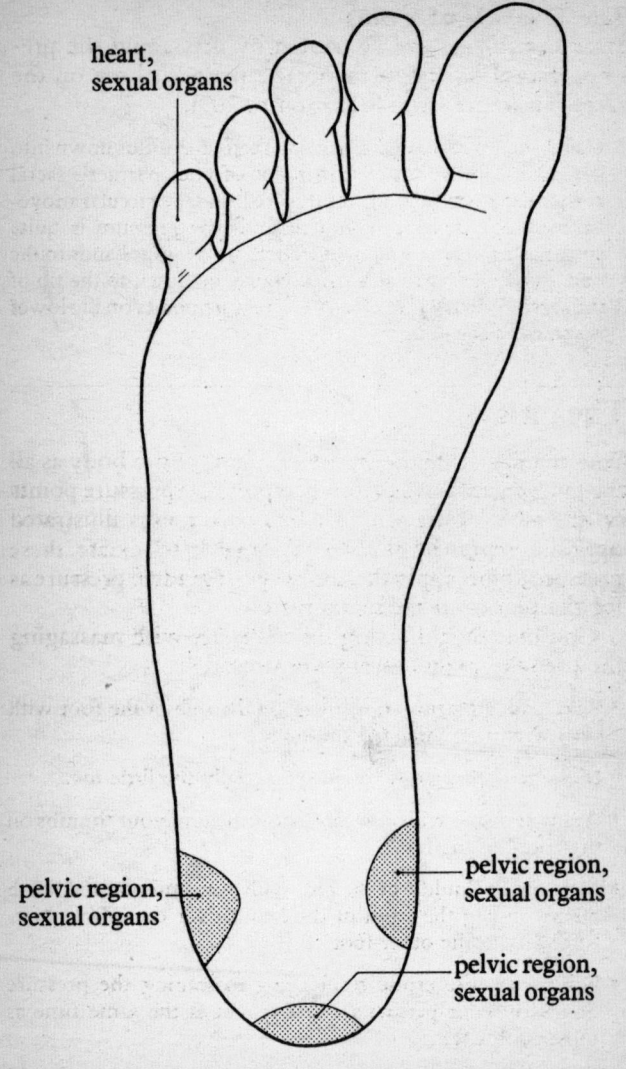

The sacrum

The Triangle of Venus
Sexual problems can be treated by massaging the pressure points on the sacral area, especially those on the sacrum triangle (see illustration p. 109).

* Using your body weight, press with your thumbs down into the small depressions on either side of your partner's sacral vertebrae. Apply a gradual pressure by a tiny circular movement of the thumbs, continue until the pressure is quite strong, then release gradually. Then, move your hands to the next sacral vertebrae and work your way down to the tip of the sacrum. Finally, massage the pressure points on the lower outsides of the sacrum.

The foot

Foot massage is highly soothing to the entire body as all the vital organs have their corresponding pressure points on the soles of the feet. The pressure points illustrated opposite represent the sexual organs; to excite these pressure points apply the same type of gradual pressure as for the points on the sacral region.

Combine the following set of strokes with massaging the pressure points to unravel stress.

* Start with a friction movement on the sole of the foot with your thumbs gliding up and down.

* Massage the toes one by one, especially the little toe.

* Apply pressure with a circular movement of your thumbs on the edges of the foot.

* Massage the middle of the foot with your thumbs and finish off by sliding the palm of the hands over the whole foot. Repeat with the other foot.

* For even more erotic results, try massaging the pressure points on your partner's sacral region at the same time as those on his feet.

15. Vitamin chart

You know you need vitamins, but do you know in which foods to find them and why you should be looking for them? Here is a brief but helpful guide to help you choose the foods you need and to understand why you need them.

Vitamin A
(Provitamin or Carotene) – fat soluble
Source: green and yellow vegetables, sprouts, dairy products, egg yolks, apricots, pumpkins, fish oil, liver.
Use: essential for normal growth and teeth formation; prevents night blindness and respiratory infections.

Vitamin B_1
(Thiamine) – can be destroyed by too much heat; water soluble
Source: vegetables, especially leafy green vegetables, whole grains, legumes, wheat germ, brewer's yeast, bananas, apples, dairy products, nuts, sprouts, liver.
Use: combats loss of appetite, indigestion and nervous irritability; essential for normal functioning of the nervous system and the digestive tract. Lack may cause constipation, diarrhoea, or beriberi.

Vitamin B_2
(Riboflavin) – heat stable, but not light stable; water soluble
Source: green leafy vegetables, citrus fruits, tomatoes, dairy products, eggs, wheatgerm, brewer's yeast, legumes, whole grains, seeds, bananas.

Use: promotes normal growth and aids in the utilization of food energy; promotes healthy skin, eyes and digestive tract. Lack may cause weakness, headaches and digestive problems.

Vitamin B3
(Niacin) – light and heat stable; water soluble
Source: whole grains, legumes, leafy greens, dairy products, brewer's yeast, wheatgerm, mushrooms, tomatoes and peanuts.
Use: utilizes food energy; essential for healthy skin and digestive tract; prevents digestive troubles and skin problems.

Vitamin B6
(Pyridoxine) – destroyed by oxidation, heat and sunlight
Source: pecans, peanuts, brewer's yeast, leafy greens, carrots, cabbage, avocados, bananas.
Use: essential in protein metabolism; helps regulate weight, prevents water storage, stabilizes emotions; helps high or low blood sugar, good for skin and teeth; prevents cramps and muscle spasms.

Vitamin B12
(Cyanocobalamin) – soluble in both alcohol and water
Source: dairy products, brewer's yeast, wheatgerm, soya beans, peanuts, seaweed.
Use: necessary for the formation of red blood cells and helpful in the prevention of anaemia.

Vitamin C
(Ascorbic Acid) – destroyed by heat and oxidation; water soluble
Source: citrus fruits (there is a day's requirements in one orange, or half a grapefruit, or one glass of juice), blackcurrants, green vegetables, tomatoes, potatoes, broccoli, cauliflower, strawberries, most melons.
Use: concerned with growth, the healing of wounds, and

with the absorption of iron into the blood; good for the skin; aids resistance to disease and infection. For healthy bones, teeth and gums; prevents scurvy and lessens the severity of colds.

Vitamin D
Source: egg yolks, liver, fatty fish, sunflower seeds, coconut, almonds, dairy products (in very small amounts), and, of course, sunshine itself.
Use: necessary for normal growth and development of the body and formation of teeth and bones; especially important for children and pregnant women.

Vitamin E
(Alpha Tocopherol) – heat stable and fat soluble
Source: leafy greens, natural oils, beets, nuts, seeds, oranges, molasses, legumes, peanuts.
Use: improves the oxygen efficiency of the muscles; thought to strengthen the reproductive system and aid the heart; good for internal and external wounds and burns; useful for pregnant women.

16. Calorie and fibre counter

(All values are per ounce (28 g) unless otherwise stated.)

	Calories	Fibre grams
Almonds, shelled, 4 oz	565	15.4
Anchovy paste, 1 tsp	14	–
Apples, 1 medium	40	2.7
Apricots, 4 oz	48	2.4
Apricots, dried, 4 oz	208	6.0
Asparagus, 4 oz	20	2.4
Avocado, ½, without dressing	125	2.1
Bacon, lean, grilled, 2 rashers	185	0.0
Banana, 1 average	65	3.4
Beans, runner, 4 oz	8	3.6
Beef, sirloin, roast, 4 oz	256	0.0
Beef, steak, grilled, 4 oz	330	0.0
Bran flakes, ½ cup	145	6.8
Bread, brown, 1 slice	51	2.6
Bread, wholemeal, 1 slice	55	4.5
Bread, rye, 1 slice	57	3.0
Broccoli, boiled, 4 oz	16	4.1
Brussels sprouts, boiled, 4 oz	20	3.3
Butter	220	0.0
Cabbage, boiled, 4 oz	8	2.8
Carrots, boiled, 4 oz	20	3.5
Cauliflower, boiled, 4 oz	10	2.0
Caviar, 1 tbsp	24	0.0
Celery, 1 large raw stick	5	1.0

	Calories	Fibre grams
Cheese: Camembert	88	0.0
Cheddar	120	0.0
cream	232	0.0
Edam	88	0.0
Gorgonzola	112	0.0
cottage	32	0.0
Chicken, roast, no bone, 4 oz	116	0.0
Chilli sauce, 1 tbsp	17	–
Cod, grilled, 4 oz	180	0.0
Crab, 4 oz	89	0.0
Cream, single, 2 tbsps (1 oz)	62	0.0
Cream, double, 2 tbsps (1 oz)	130	0.0
Cucumber, 4 oz	20	0.6
Dates, dried	60	2.4
Eggs, boiled, 1	80	0.0
Eggs, plain omelette, 2 eggs	212	0.0
Figs, green, 4 oz	48	2.8
Figs, dried, 4 oz	244	0.8
French dressing, 1 tbsp	86	0.0
Grapefruit, ½	18	0.5
Ham, fresh/smoked, 4 oz	338	0.0
Honey, 1 tbsp	60	–
Ice-cream, 2 oz	100	–
Lamb chop, grilled, 4 oz	310	0.0
Lamb, leg, roasted, 4 oz	332	0.0
Leeks, boiled, 4 oz	28	4.4
Lemon, medium	20	1.0
Lemon/lime juice, 1 tbsp	5	0.0
Lettuce, 2 leaves	7	0.2
Liver, 4 oz	180	0.0
Lobster, 2 oz	78	0.0
Macaroni, boiled, 4 oz	128	1.7
Mackerel, 8 oz	305	0.0
Melon, 4-oz slice	15	0.5
Milk, whole, ½ pint	160	0.0
Milk, skimmed, ½ pint	100	0.0
Mushrooms, 4 oz	36	2.5

	Calories	Fibre grams
Mussels, shelled	25	0.0
Nuts, mixed, 4 oz	371	4.0
Oils, 1 tbsp	124	0.0
Onions, 4 oz	15	1.5
Onions, spring	10	–
Orange, 1 average	40	3.4
Oysters, 6	200	0.0
Peaches, 1 whole	36	1.4
Pears, 1 medium	36	2.5
Pepper, green/red	16	1.3
Pineapple, 1 slice	26	0.8
Potatoes, baked, 1 medium	96	5.7
Potatoes, roast, 2 small	140	2.0
Potatoes, boiled, 4 oz	84	1.8
Prawns, peeled	30	0.0
Prunes, dried, 4 oz	76	15.2
Rabbit, stewed, 4 oz	104	0.0
Raisins	70	1.0
Raspberries, 4 oz	28	8.4
Rice, boiled, 2 oz	70	1.2
Salmon, steamed, 4 oz	228	0.0
Salmon, smoked, 4 oz	178	0.0
Salmon, canned, 4 oz	156	0.0
Sardines, drained, 8 oz	171	0.0
Shrimps, 4 oz	128	0.0
Soup, consommé, ½ pint	40	–
Soup, vegetable, ½ pint	126	8.0
Spaghetti, cooked, 4 oz	155	1.7
Spinach, 4 oz	28	7.1
Strawberries, 4 oz	28	2.5
Sugar, brown, 1 tbsp	45	–
Tomato, 1 medium	8	0.8
Tongue (beef), 4 oz	160	0.0
Trout, grilled, 4 oz	100	0.0
Tuna fish, tinned, 2 oz	135	0.0
Water-ice, 1 scoop	236	–
Wheatgerm, 2 tbsp	35	0.3

	Calories	Fibre grams
Wheat flakes	125	2.6
Wholewheat spaghetti, cooked, 4oz	155	5.7
Yoghurt, natural, 1 small carton	75	0.0

Drinks

	Calories	Fibre grams
Brandy, 1½ oz (38 ml)	120	
Champagne, 1 glass	90	
Fruit juice, 4 oz	48	1.0
Gin, 1½ oz	120	
Port, 1½ oz	90	
Rum, 1½ oz	105	
Sherry, 1 glass	85	
Whisky, 1½ oz	110	
Wine, dry, 1 glass	85	
Wine, sweet, 1 glass	100	

17. List of suppliers

Fruit and vegetables

Markets:

Portobello Rd, London W11
Berwick St, Soho, London W1
Church St, London W9
Shepherd's Bush, London W12
Brixton Rd, London SW9

} offer a wide range of tropical fruits

Others:

Robert Bruce, near Covent Garden ⊖ London WC2. Truffles and different types of vegetables, mushrooms, dandelion roots, mangoes, kiwi fruit, fennel and passion fruit.

The Thai Shop, Craven Terrace, London W2. A wide range of fresh, exotic fruit and vegetables flown in from Thailand: papaya ripe and unripe, limes, pumpkin, fresh chillies, ginger root, coriander leaves, fresh or pulped tamarind, dried fish, etc.

Tropical Fruits, 29 and 63 Queensway, London W2. Tropical fruit in season and more ordinary fruit and vegetables.

Clifton Fruiterers, 4 Clifton Rd, London W9. Specialists in continental fruit and vegetables.

Continental and oriental stores and delicatessens

Walton Hassel and Port Ltd, 88 High St, London N6. Unusual international foods, range of European cheeses.

Kasmir Store, 16 Kenway Rd, London SW5. Oriental grocery, excellent range of spices.

Asian Stores, 58 Moscow Rd, London W2. Asian spices.

Athenian Grocery, 16 Moscow Rd, London W2. Middle Eastern food shop, wide range of spices.

Mr Christian's, 11 Elgin Crescent, London W11. Continental delicatessen, wide range of cold meats, salamis, pâté, etc.

Health foods

Ceres Bakery & Health Foods, 269a Portobello Rd, London W11. Wholemeal breads, natural foods, organically grown vegetables, pulses, etc.

Neal's Yard Wholefood Warehouse, 2 Neal's Yard, Covent Garden, London WC2. Nuts, grains, pulses, seeds, etc.

Butchers

W. Fenn Ltd, 27 Frith St, London W1. Stock poultry and all kinds of game including venison, veal, quail.

Fishmongers

Martins 202 and Smiths 208, Portobello Rd, London W11. Foreign fish like octopus, calamar, squid.

Rudman, 71 High St, Wimbledon SW19. Fresh fish in season, shellfish, game and poultry.

John Gow, 55 Moscow Rd, London W2. Live and cooked lobster, crab.

R. Rowe & Son Ltd, 243 Camden High St, London NW1. Marvellous fish shop with live and cooked crab and a wide range of fish.

Leadenhall Market, London EC3. Fish and live lobsters.

Richards (Soho) Ltd, 11 Brewer St, London W1. English and Continental fishmongers.

Chinese supermarkets

Loon Fung Supermarket, 42–43 Gerard St, London W1.

Great Wall Supermarket, 31–37 Wardour St, London W1.

Hong Kong Supermarket, 93–107 Shaftesbury Ave, London W1.

Peking Store, 11 Porchester Rd, London W2.

Wing Hing Loon, 46 Faulkner St, Manchester 1.

Large supermarkets such as Safeway now stock a wide range of tropical and continental fruit, vegetables, cheese and other foods. Large stores, for example, Harrods and Selfridges, also sell fresh fish and shellfish, game, poultry, cold meats and groceries at reasonable prices.

Essential oils

The Body Shop, 203 Kensington High St, London W8 and 8 Blenheim Crescent, London W11, and 1A White Hart Lane, London SW13.

The Morlé Swimming and Beauty Centre, 176 Kensington High St, London W8.

18. Weights and measures

Liquid measurements

British	American	Metric
1 pint = 20 oz	= 1¼ pints = 2½ cups	= 6 dl
½ pint = 10 oz	= 1¼ cups	= 3 dl
¼ pint = 5 oz	= ½ cup plus 2 tablespoons	= 1.5 dl
2 oz = 4 tablespoons	= ¼ cup	= 50 ml
1 tablespoon = ½ oz	= ½ oz	= 15 ml
1 teaspoon = ¼ tablespoon		= 5 ml

Solid measurements

British	American	Metric
1 lb = 16 oz	approx. 2 cups	400 grammes
½ lb = 8 oz	approx. 1 cup	200 grammes
¼ lb = 4 oz	approx. ½ cup	100 grammes
1 oz butter	approx. 2 tablespoons	25 grammes

Oven temperatures

Gas	Degrees farenheit	Degrees centigrade
low	200	100
¼	225	110
½	250	120
1	275	140
2	300	150
3	325	160
4	350	180
5	375	190
6	400	200
7	425	220
8	450	230
9	475	240

Index

alfalfa: Elixir of life, 89
alfalfa sprouts, 22, 27
almonds, 25
amino acids, 13, 20, 22
alcohol: as an aphrodisiac, 88 see also cocktails
aphrodisiacs, 11–17; and alcohol, 88; essential oils as, 107; for men, 32; no longer in use, 12; in tisanes, 89–90
Aphrodite, 12, 14
apple: Eve's ice, 82; Sweet sensation, 86
asparagus, 13, 21, 34; Asparagus and smoked ham rolls, 62; Suggestion omelette, 58–9
aubergines: Angela's aubergine chutney, 56; Lobster in aubergine, 66
avocado: Dream avocado, 51; Fiery avocado, 51; Suitor's salad, 54

bamboo shoots: Hot and sour soup, 42–3
banana, 35; A taste of honey and, 86; Banana, honey and nut spread, 63; Caribbean sundae, 83
bean sprouts, 21, 22, 35; Lovers salad, 52 see also alfalfa, lentils, etc.
beef: Ginger beef, 78–9; Soup of beef with lovage, 39; Steak au poivre, 79–80; Steak tartare, 80; Tipsy steak, 78
blood pressure: high, 14, 20
breakfast: blender breakfasts, 36; importance of, 33; muesli, 36; what to eat, 33 see also brunch
brewers yeast, 19, 25, 35, 36
broccoli, 17, 34
brown rice, 35
brunch, 37
buttermilk, 37

calorie counter, 115–18
carp: Crafty carp in aspic, 70
carrot: Smooth carrot soup, 44; Sunkissed carrots, 53
Casanova, 16, 17, 37
cauliflower, 35; Choufleur à la grecque, 50; Surprise salad, 53
caviar, 13, 14; on toast with lemon juice, 37
celery, 13, 14, 34
cellulite, 22, 27
chicken: Chicken exotica, 72; Chicken paprika, 73; Chicken unforgettable, 74; Haunting chicken, 73; Spring-love chicken, 72
cholesterol, 14
chutney: Angela's aubergine chutney, 56; Deceptive chutney, 55–6; Love-apple chutney, 55; Luscious lime chutney, 57; Outrageous orange chutney, 57
cider vinegar, 19
cocktails, 92–4
corn oil, 17
cottage cheese: with garlic and chives, 63; with prawns and chives, 62
crab, 31; Aphrodite's bouillon, 46; Paradise crab, 68

dairy products, 25, 26
dancing: African, 104, 105; belly, 104; benefits of, 104–5
desserts: A taste of honey, 86; Banana split, 83; Caribbean sundae, 83; Crème renversée à la indienne, 87; Eastern delight, 87; Eve's ice, 82; Lovers' dream salads, nos 1–5, 84; Mango and gin sorbet, 82; Passionate dreams, 85; Spiced grapefruit, 85–6; Succulent sorbet, 82; Sweet sensations, 86; What-the-hell parfait, 82–3
diet: attitude to, 18, 19; the High Sexuality Diet: foods to eat on, 33, 34, 35; foods to avoid on, 34; principles of, 33; slimming on, 19, 27, 29, 32, 34
dieting: adverse affects of, 7–8
diuretics, 13, 22
drinks: cocktails, 92–4: non-alcoholic, 94; for breakfast, 36; for health and beauty, 29–30; punches, 91; spirits *see* cocktails; tisanes, 89–90

eels: Elusive eels, 71
eggs, 17, 20, 26; Eastern delight, 87; Enchanting cloud omelette, 58; hard boiled, with anchovy fillets and mushrooms, 62; Suggestion omelette, 58–9
exercise, 28, 95–101; importance of, 95–6
exercises, 96–101 *see also* yoga
eyes, 26

fats, 14; polyunsaturated, 20, 21, 22, 32; saturated, 25
fennel: Surprise salad, 53
fennel seeds, 11
fibre, 20, 21, 23; in High Sexuality Diet, 32
fibre counter, 115–18
Fish: Canapés aux poissons, 50; Neptune salad, 60–1 *see also* carp, eel, salmon, trout, etc.
fruit, 25, 26, 27, 35; Caribbean sundae, 83; Charm nectar, 89; juice, 35; salads, 84–6; suppliers, 119 *see also* apple, banana, etc.

game, 32, 34 *see* partridge, pheasant, pigeon, quail etc.
garlic, 14, 35
ginger, 35; Blast of passion, 89; Ginger beef, 78–9
ginseng, 11, 12, 15, 35; Blast of Passion, 89; oil, 107
grapefruit: Spiced grapefruit, 85–6

ham: Asparagus and smoked ham rolls, 62; with horseradish and carrot, 62
hair, 25
hare: Roast saddle of hare, 75–6
herbs, 35
honey, 11, 12, 15–16, 35, 36; A taste of honey, 86
hormones: pheromones, 14, 17
hors-d'oeuvres: Canapés aux poissons, 50; Canapés ronds aux crevettes, 49; Choufleur à la grecque, 50; Dream avocado, 51; Fiery avocado, 51; Perk-you-up prawns, 49; Venus shell, 48–9

impotence, 17; how to treat it, 108
infusions *see* tisanes
inositol, 20

kelp, 20, 32
kiwi fruits, 21

lecithin, 20, 22, 27, 36
lentil sprouts, 22
lentils, 25, 26, 35; Spicy red lentil soup, 42; Wonder broth, 39–40
lettuce, 17, 26; Honeymoon salad, 54
lime: Luscious lime chutney, 57; Miracle mackerel with lime, 60
linoleic acid, 22
liquorice root, 11; Charm nectar, 89
liver, 20, 26, 32, 34; calf's: Cupid's casserole, 78
lobster: Island salad, 54–5; Lobster in aubergines, 66; Lobster in style, 64; Saucy but nice, 65; Temptress bisque, 46–7; Understated grill, 54–5
lovage: Soup of beef with, 39
love apples *see* tomatoes
lunches, 58–63; foods to include, 33

mackerel: Miracle mackerel with lime, 60
main meals, 64–80; foods to include, 33 *see also* beef, chicken, etc.
mangoes, 21; Mango and gin sorbet, 82
Marquis de Sade, 12, 17
massage, 106–11; essential oils used in, 107; pressure points, 111; shiatsu, 107; treatment of sexual problems, 111
melon: juicy melon salad, 52
minerals, 13, 14, 20, 22, 25, 26; calcium, 13, 14, 21, 26; iodine, 20, 27; iron, 21, 22, 23, 25; magnesium, 21, 32; phosphorus, 13, 14, 20, 21, 26, 31; potassium, 13, 14, 21, 22; sulphur, 26; zinc, 21, 22, 23; deficiency of, 16
molasses, 21, 25
muesli, 33; concoctions for breakfast, 36
mushrooms, 34; Chinese: Hot and sour soup, 42–3; Wild mushroom soup, 45
mussels: Gorgeous black mussel soup, 45–6; Persuasion mussels, 67
mustard seed sprouts, 22

nails, 26
natural foods, 18–23, 24
nutrients, 16, 20, 23, 27
nuts, 17, 20, 21, 26, 37

octopus: Deep sea daube, 68–9
oils: essential oils used in massage, 107–8; from seeds, 32, 107–8; salad, 34; suppliers of, 120 *see also* sesame, sunflower, etc.
onions, 34; and potato soup, 40–1
orange, 21, 35; outrageous orange chutney, 57
ox-tongue: in aspic, 61
oysters, 12, 16; and lemon slices, 37

papaya, 21; Hidden charms, 77; Papaya sensation, 93
parsley, 21, 35

partridge: Pleasure
    partridges, 75
passion fruit: Caribbean
    sundae, 83; Passionate
    dreams, 85
peaches, 16, 35; Passionate
    dreams, 85; Sparkling
    peach nectar, 93
pheasant: salmi, 76
pigeon: Consommé
    Rasputin, 38; Tender
    pigeon soup, 40
pineapple: Caribbean sundae,
    83
pollen, 16
potatoes, 26, 34; Irresistible
    baked potatoes, 60–1;
    Onion and potato soup,
    40–1
prawns, 31; Canapés ronds
    aux crevettes, 49;
    Perk-you-up prawns, 49;
    Prawns rougaille, 66;
    Sesame prawns, 67; Sweet
    nothing prawns, 67; with
    cottage cheese and chives,
    62
pressure points, 111
prostate glands, 16–17
protein, 17, 19, 21, 22, 23
pulses: Golden
    mulligatawny, 41 see also
    lentils, etc
pumpkin: Cinderella's soup,
    45; Tender hearts, 43;
    Wonder broth, 39
pumpkin seeds, 16–17, 35;
    Lover's salad, 52
punches, 91

quails: grilled, 62

rabbit: Magic rabbit, 74 see
    also hare
Rabelais, 17

raspberries: What-the-hell
    parfait, 82–3
roe, 14: Sea-urchin: fried with
    chives and lemon juice, 37;
    on crackers, 37; steamed,
    37; soft herring: with
    watercress, 62; sturgeon see
    caviar
roughage see fibre

sago: Eastern delight, 87
safflower oil, 17, 22
salad oil, 34
salads: Honeymoon salad, 54;
    Island salad, 54–5; Juicy
    melon salad, 52; Neptune's
    salad, 60–1; Suitor's salad,
    54; Sunkissed carrots, 53;
    Surprise salad, 53
Salmon: Suitor's salad, 54;
    with shallots, lemon juice
    and truffles, 62; Venus
    shell, 48–9
sandwiches, 63
sardines: Scintillating sardines
    with love apples, 60; with
    cheese, onion and
    tomatoes, 62
sauces: Stimulating sauce, 56
seafoods, 27, 31, 35 see
    mussels, prawns, tuna, etc.
seeds, 21–2; Elixir of life, 89
    see also sesame, sunflower,
    etc.
sesame seeds, 11, 22; Elixir of
    life, 89; Sesame prawns, 67
sesamol, 22
shellfish: on High Sexuality
    Diet, 32 see crab, lobster,
    mussels, etc
shiatsu see massage
shrimps: Deceptive chutney,
    55–6; Golden dream
    shrimps, 68; Potent potted
    shrimps, 59

127

skin 25–6
snacks: bedside, 62; sandwiches, 63
soups: Aphrodite's bouillon, 46; Cinderella's soup, 45; Consommé Rasputin, 38; Golden mulligatawny, 41; Onion and potato soup, 40–1; Smooth carrot soup, 44; Soup of beef with lovage, 39; Spectacular bouillon, 44; Spicy red lentil soup, 42; Temptress bisque, 46; Tender hearts, 43; Tender-pigeon soup, 40; Wild mushroom soup, 45; Wonder broth, 40
soya beans, 20, 22, 35
soya oil, 22
spaghetti: à la Don Juan, 76–7
Spanish Fly, 12
spices, 35
spinach, 26, 34; Lover's salad, 52; Spectacular bouillon, 44
spirits, 93 *see also* cocktails
spreads: for sandwiches, 63
sprouts, 25 *see also* lentils, soya beans, etc.
squid: Martin's marinated squid, 69
stimulation, 13, 15, 35
strawberries, 21; Lovers' dream salad, 84; Succulent sorbet, 81
stress, 27
stretch marks, 26
sunflower oil, 17, 22, 35
sunflower seeds, 17, 21
supplementary foods, 18–23
suppliers, 119–21

teas *see* tisanes
tisanes, 89–90
tomatoes, 26, 34; Love-apple chutney, 55; Scintillating sardines with love apples, 60
trout: Canapés aux poissons, 50; Extravagant trout, 70
truffles, 13, 17, 34; Enchanting cloud omelette, 58
tuna: with tamarind, 71

vegetable juice, 35
vegetable oils *see* sesame, sunflower etc.
vegetables, 20, 26 *see also* carrot, cauliflower etc.
vitality, 28
vitamin chart, 112–14
Vitamin A, 20, 26, 29, 32; B, 14, 19, 20; B Complex, 21, 23, 25, 26, 27, 29; C, 14, 21, 26, 27, 29; D, 20, 32; E, 16, 17, 20, 21, 23, 26, 32; F, 20; K, 20, 32

water, 22–3, 25, 27, 35; mineral, 23, 35
watercress, 26, 34; and soft herring roes, 62; Spectacular bouillon, 44; Suitor's salad, 54
weights and measures, 122–3
wheatgerm, 17, 23, 35
whole grains, 20, 23, 32; cereals, 17, 20, 25 *see also* muesli
wholemeal bread, 17, 20, 23, 25, 32, 35
wine, 34
winkles, 31–2
wrinkles: how to prevent, 26

yoga: importance of, 101–2; positions, 102–4 *see also* exercise